married, with two grown-up children. *Because I'm Bella* is his first
novel for Oxf

D0610742

Because I'm Bella

Because I'm Bella

Joe Hackett

OXFORD
UNIVERSITY PRESS

OXFORD

UNIVERSITY PRESS

Great Clarendon Street, Oxford OX2 6DP

Oxford University Press is a department of the University of Oxford.
It furthers the University's objective of excellence in research, scholarship,
and education by publishing worldwide in

Oxford New York

Auckland Bangkok Buenos Aires
Cape Town Chennai Dar es Salaam Delhi Hong Kong Istanbul
Karachi Kolkata Kuala Lumpur Madrid Melbourne Mexico City Mumbai
Nairobi São Paulo Shanghai Taipei Tokyo Toronto

Oxford is a registered trade mark of Oxford University Press
in the UK and in certain other countries

British Library Cataloguing in Publication Data available

ISBN 0 19 275334 7

1 3 5 7 9 10 8 6 4 2

Typeset by AFS Image Setters Ltd, Glasgow

Printed in Great Britain

One

First, I dreamed that I stole a young child—a boy, with lovely brown hair and a golden-brown skin. Then, only a few weeks later, I really did it.

My dream was just getting to a happy ending. Happy endings are not real—they only come in dreams and stories, especially stories for children. 'Then they all lived happily ever after.' That's the ending to a story for children. That's what little children want to hear, to give them security.

When they got older, like me, into double figures and almost a teenager, they began to know different.

In my dream everything was all smiles and warm sunshine. The little boy, about three years old, clung on tight to my hand, grateful to have been stolen, glad to be with me. He kept asking me things, and I felt important. I noticed that he was wearing little red shoes.

Then, suddenly, I was woken by a soft knock at my door. It was a new cleaning lady at the Home where I had to live with the other children whose parents didn't want them, or couldn't manage them, or had harmed them.

She opened my door cautiously, as if I might attack her.

'Oh, hello. Excuse me, please. Can I come in, my love?

Is that OK with you, lover? You're Bella, aren't you? My name is Mrs Bloor.'

'Go away,' I mumbled from under my pillow, still half-asleep. 'We don't use surnames here. I've got to call you by your Christian name. It's meant to make everything more friendly, or something.' I opened one eye and looked at her.

'Oh. OK. My name is Tina, then. Can I do your room?' When she smiled I saw that she was missing a tooth, top left four.

She was nice and too polite. It made me want to be rude, especially as she had woken me when I was enjoying the build-up to the happy ending.

'No. I'm still in bed, can't you see? I was having a dream.' I was really annoyed to have been woken up. I wanted to remember how I had stolen the little boy, and who he was and how I met him and where we were, and how it would end and everything.

'Oh, well, I can come back later, my love. In half an hour?' She was only about 30 but she behaved like an old lady—all good manners and kindness. I hated it when she called me 'my love'. All that west country stuff. I'm not anybody's love.

'I suppose so. Come back in twenty minutes.' I was still under my pillow, and said it so that she could only half-hear me. I liked to mumble. I knew how annoying it could be.

'Is everything all right, Bella?'

'That's a stupid question. Very stupid. Of course everything's not all right. This is a Children's Residential Home. It's for unhappy children. Didn't they tell you?'

'Oh, I see. But is there anything particular today? You look like you lost a pound and found sixpence.'

I didn't know what sixpence was, but I wasn't going to say. I decided to trick her. I got out from under the pillow, and stared hard at her.

'I'm always miserable. Haven't they told you? I want to win the Annual Miserable Competition. We have it at Christmas, which is meant to be a happy time, only it isn't. Christmas is only a few months away, so I'm getting into training. My rival in the Annual Miserable Competition is Anthony, the boy in the end room. Have you met him yet? The one who looks like a floppy white cushion, with dents in it.'

'That's not very nice, my love. No, I haven't met him yet.' Tina was now standing quite close, leaning on her broom, and I could smell her cheap perfume. It's one you buy at Woolworth's.

'It's true. He's all floppy like a beanbag. He's one of us fat ones. He hardly ever comes out of his room and hardly ever says anything. You can hear him crying at night-time. He's only been here six weeks.'

'Oh, dear. Oh, I say. The poor little chap.'

Secretly, I quite liked it that she was sorry for Anthony, but I was still suspicious of her.

'Why do you want to work here? They don't pay much.'

'The hours suit me. I can come here after I get my oldest boy, Tony, to school and the younger one, Tarik, to playgroup and then I just get the two and a half hours cleaning here before going to collect Tarik again and take him home for his dinner.'

'Where did he get his name?'

'He's named after his dad. His dad's Egyptian. He hardly knows him.'

'Like me. My dad's in the nick, long gone, and I haven't seen my mum for ages, now. She's completely mental. She's got Munchausen's. Have you heard of it?'

Tina looked blank.

'It's not the one when they make their children ill, so then they get attention. No, she did it to herself. Made *herself* ill. Kept doing it. Even pretended she was dying. It was all pretend. That's why they took me away, in the end. It was too dramatic for me . . . no, that's not the word.'

'Traumatic, my love?'

'Yes. They tried foster parents for me but that didn't work, not when I kept acting up and arguing with them, so now I'm here.'

'Maybe you'll hear from your mum at Christmas, Bella.' Tina was upset for me.

'I doubt it. She hasn't written all year. Why should she bother now?' I liked to talk badly about my mum, as if I didn't care. But I still wanted to see her one day, when I finally ran away from the Home, which I was planning to do, quite soon. 'No, I'm definitely going to win the Annual Miserable Competition this year. Unless Anthony has got some new bit of misery he hasn't shown us yet.'

'What's the prize?' She believed me. I had her hooked.

'You get your face painted as a sad clown and you go to the circus.'

'Really? Oh, I say.'

'Yes, really. Everyone in this dump knows that.'

She'd believe anything, that Tina. Miserable Competition! Sad Clown! Circus! When she found out I'd lied to her I supposed she'd be cross and would feel silly for believing me. She tried to look into my eyes but I kept them down.

I stuck my head back under the pillow and tried to finish my dream. I wanted to hold the little boy's hand again, and know that he loved me, even though I had stolen him. That's all I wanted, for him to love me, and for him to be just mine, nobody else's. I wanted to have the happy ending. But I couldn't, because I couldn't go back to sleep again.

Tina went to do Maddie's room. I thought they'd get on well. She'd like Maddie, who's pretty, dark-haired, interesting-looking, and slim and more like a girl should be. A proper teenage girl, looking older than her age. Not stuck in time and stuck in the wrong body, like me.

I was one of the six fat ones in the Home. There were eight children, and only two were thin. I hadn't a clue how they stayed like that. They ate the same food as us fatties. It wasn't fair. Life is not fair, is what the staff said.

Whenever I said something wasn't fair they just shrugged and said life's tough. As if they knew anything. They should have had to live in the Home, like us, not just come there to work. They'd got places to go back to, and families. We didn't. We didn't have anywhere else to live. It was this, or nothing. Or running away.

It would have been fun to put them in a Home and then come to visit them and tell them what to do. Then they'd know. They'd have to wear suits, and brush their hair. They'd hate that. Oh, yes, and there'd be a rule about no smoking. They'd hate that, too, because some of them smoke like chimneys. Then I'd say they couldn't have any booze or TV, either, just when they had stopped complaining about the no-smoking rule. I'd watch their grown-up faces very closely. Which would mean having to look at their horrible whiskers. I'm talking about the women workers. At least the men shaved.

They'd stamp their feet and hit the tables with their fists. Then they'd say, in their caring social-work voices, 'That's not fair!' and I'd laugh and laugh.

Then they'd look at me and say something like, 'That's no way for a twelve year old to behave. You're getting a big girl now, Bella,' but Bella's only the name my mother gave me, and I wanted to change it. Being called 'beautiful' in Italian was a sick joke, when you saw my

5

face. One eye is light blue and one is light green, which makes me a freak, and my nose is too red and short.

Soon I'd have been in the Home for six months and they still hadn't found me another family to have just for myself, to give me another try, seeing as I couldn't visit my mother. She was locked up somewhere hundreds of miles away, in Yorkshire. I'd never been there. She was a danger to herself and to me, that's what the file said. It was two inches thick. All my grisly details are in there. The ones you probably want to know about. It mentions something called my 'poor body image'.

It wasn't just that I was fat. I was tall, too. I was the biggest girl in my year. Once, in the school playground, I heard a boy call me 'The Whale', behind my back. I decked him. I learned to punch from my dad—before they put him in jail. I hit the boy with a right-hander, quick and hard. I spun on my left foot, 180 degrees, and hit him in the eye. I wish it had been his nose. Then there'd have been lots of blood.

I was starving. I went down to the kitchen to cadge a late breakfast from the cook. For us emotionally starved children, the kitchen should have been 'the warm, beating heart of the Home'—that's what my old social worker used to say, she uses words like that. She was quite fat herself.

Instead, it was a nasty room. A room with a door at each end, so it was like a wide corridor. It was painted a shiny cream colour—the colour of weak custard, which was the only kind they served up, and there was a white fridge and white cupboard. Lots of white surfaces. It was more like a hospital than a kitchen. There was metal, plastic everywhere, all cold to the touch. Too shiny. The windows got condensation, so you couldn't see out.

6

The oven was brown and electric. Its dials were complicated and you didn't want to touch them.

Someone had put up a notice warning about junk foods. There were at least three other warning notices about food hygiene, about keeping sharp knives under lock and key (in case we disturbed children got our murderous little mitts on them, but it doesn't say that), and about having to wash your hands before you make meals.

You don't get notices on the walls in a real family home, do you? You don't get star charts pinned up on the walls, so that everyone can see how you have been behaving. You don't get notices above the washing machines, saying 'Not to be used without staff supervision', or in the bathrooms saying 'Only one child at a time allowed to use this room', and all sorts of other notices saying do this, don't do that.

There were locks on the lavatories but only dinky little silver ones, so that we couldn't barricade ourselves in. We weren't allowed locks on our bedroom doors. There was nowhere you could get away from the other kids. Then, there were the smells—a bit sour, a mixture of dirty knickers or pants and overcooked cabbage—and the noise, because everybody had their own ghetto blasters.

If it wasn't that, it was the noise from the computer where the boys played racing car games, with all the sounds of the crashes and screeching tyres. Oh, and you were allowed to choose the colour of the paint in your own room, but everywhere else the Home was painted in shades of washable yellow, which is not my favourite colour. We had Buttercup and Marigold and Primrose. Totally yucksome.

It was like I was not allowed to be myself, in the Home, especially in the kitchen. It wasn't a nice room. Nobody would say it was a nice room. Yet we children went there again and again, looking for magic food to make us happy. To give us a happy ending. Our whiny little voices were like Oliver Twist's. 'Please can we have some more, sir?'

We deserved more, but we never seemed to get it. Never.

Two

Like I said, you got no peace in the Home.

Just after I was rid of Tina and had gone back to my room from the kitchen (with a big chicken and mayonnaise sandwich, because I'd missed breakfast) Anthony came knocking at my door. I stuffed the sandwich under my bedspread.

He was apologetic as usual. 'Sorry to bother you, Bella,' he said.

I gave him a cool look—the one I practised in the mirror, copying it from a girls' magazine. 'What do you want?'

'Have you seen my fluffy?'

Anthony kept a truly sad fluffy toy in his bedroom. Once, it was bright red and yellow, and was a bird. Not too bad to look at, maybe. Some kind of parrot. Now, it was a muddy orange colour, and shapeless, with no beak. The colours ran when the staff took it away from him and shoved it in the washing machine because it was so filthy from him mauling it and cuddling it all the time with his dirty, sweaty hands.

I told him I hadn't seen it. It's his favourite thing. He's truly sad.

His fat face quivered like a white jelly with two green fruit gums in it—his eyes. 'I've asked everyone else if they've seen him. All the other kids said they hadn't. I was hoping you had him.'

'Why would I have it? It's completely disgusting,' I said.

That did it. He began to cry. Two big tears welled up in the corners of each eye and trickled down his cheeks, and then there were two more. They were silent tears. He didn't sob, or shake. He just stood there and stared at me through his tears. I'd done the worst thing ever. I had insulted his fluffy. I took pity on him. I had to. I softened my voice.

'I expect it'll turn up. When did you last see it?'

'After breakfast. I tucked him up . . . ' (it was a male, the fluffy, although you couldn't tell) '. . . under my pillow, as usual. When I came back, after my go on the computer, he was gone. I'm sure someone has stolen him, just to be horrible.' People were always being horrible to Anthony, but he asked for it, if you want my opinion. He never stood up for himself.

I had an idea. 'Have you asked the new cleaner, Mrs Bloor? Her name's Tina.'

'I didn't know we had a new cleaner.'

'She started today. She's doing Maddie's room now, can't you hear the Hoover?'

He ran off down the corridor, surprisingly quickly for a boy so blubbery.

I couldn't help being curious. I stuck my head out from my room and saw the touching scene of Anthony being reunited with his horrible fluffy. Tina Bloor begged his forgiveness. She had tidied up his room while he was on the computer and put the fluffy in a top cupboard. No one had told her how precious the fluffy was, and how it had to stay under Anthony's pillow during the day. In five minutes Anthony came back, all smiles.

'Thanks, Bella,' he said. By this time Maddie was in my room. We were breaking one of the rules, and getting away with it. We were not meant to be in our rooms unless we were alone. Today the staff were having a meeting, downstairs (they have loads of meetings) and hadn't noticed us. I had to ask Anthony in, rather than have him stand in the corridor, where he would be seen.

In a minute Maddie, who liked to think she was in charge, just because she was oldest, was telling us about her latest fantasy boyfriend. We usually listened to her stories, because they were quite entertaining, but we never believed them. Like, no one had ever seen her with a boy. Mind you, she was quite pretty, with her long brown hair and nice complexion. She'd never had spots. She had started to wear eye-liner and lipstick, too, and she was getting to be the shape girls should be, not a blob like yours truly.

She was carrying her white fake-leather bag. It was bulging with make-up stuff. 'Is one of my eyebrows pointing upwards?' she asked. I said it wasn't, but she had to fetch out her little mirror to have a look. She was wearing her high shoes today, to make her taller, the ones with the cork heels, all laced up with black plastic string, tied high up her ankle. She had on a black miniskirt split at the thigh, and this was also laced up with black plastic string. She wore a white top with a low neckline to reveal her little boobs—all the top of them, with the V of the neckline plunging between. The white top was cropped short so that you could see her belly button, with its glass bead. Her tummy was all brown, from the tanning cream she used.

Her brown hair was very straight, down to her shoulders. She wore a tarty gold chain round her throat, and a pendant, too. Did she know what effect this would have on boys? You bet she did. Did she know how jealous

I felt, because I was a barrel and she was a curvy stick of spaghetti? Probably not. I don't think she thought about other girls—only boys. She had a baby voice, all soft and sweet, and she'd read all the teenage magazines, with the articles about how to get boyfriends.

Anthony, Maddie, and I were all teenagers, or almost. Then there was a big gap down to the other children, who were all nine and ten. We hated them.

Anthony began complaining about how one of them had eaten the last of the cereals. I said that another one was being too cheeky again—she looked like a drowned rat and had got a mouth on her like a sewer and would just stand there and insult you with interesting swear words. I didn't know the meaning of some of them, to be honest. Then Maddie said that the other one, the littlest, had wet himself again and hadn't changed his trousers, and that he stank.

'We're too old to be in the same Home as them,' Maddie said. She'd a London accent. I agreed with her, and so did Anthony. We'd said all this to the staff, ages ago, but they didn't listen. All they would say was that there was nowhere else for us to go. Meaning, no one wanted us.

Anthony, who was quite clever, had sat down on my bed, making a big round dent, but now he stood up and said he had an idea. 'A gang. Let's have a proper, old-fashioned gang, like in the old comic books,' he said.

Maddie looked doubtful. She always did, if it was someone else's idea. 'What sort of a gang?' she said.

'We could do new things, and stuff,' Anthony said, vaguely. 'Like, play horrible tricks on the little ones, and go down town together. We could be the Big Three.'

'Big Two, more like,' said Maddie, sneering. She was referring to Anthony's and my weight, of course. Because she was the only other older girl in the Home, I had to be friends with her, even when she said nasty things like that about me.

I looked out of the window, avoiding her. The Home was on the edge of a village, next to a farm. There were red Devon cows the colour of conkers out in the fields, and their calves. The west country hills, with woods at their tops, sloped up to the moors. There were clouds blowing in from the Atlantic, further over to the west. It looked like it was going to rain.

I didn't think Anthony's idea was very brilliant, and he was vague about what he meant, but the long winter was coming, and we'd be stuck in this dump and we had to think of something, especially if we could be naughty and get away with it. Instead of being nasty back to Maddie, I took Anthony's side. Soon, we started planning what we would do. Maddie joined in. When we let her be the leader, and started writing up all the rules and secret signs of our membership, and where to leave secret messages for each other and how to communicate by hand signals and special winks so that the staff wouldn't know, well, she got quite enthusiastic.

A few days later, Tina invited me to her house. I suppose she was sorry for me. I wasn't expecting it. I hadn't tried to be nice to her, or anything.

'Come to tea, my lover. Come and meet my little Tarik, you'll like him,' she said. So I went, because I hadn't anything else to do that afternoon. She didn't live far away. One of the new houses, hardly bigger than a dog kennel, at the end of the village.

She was very proud of her two boys, Tony and Tarik. Tony, who was a snotty-nosed six year old, skinny, with mousy hair, already into being the next David Beckham, came running in from school and running straight out again, dribbling his football. I wasn't interested in him at all.

But Tarik. He was lovely. Straightaway, I fell in love with his big brown eyes and his coffee skin and his crinkly dark copper hair. I know you can't fall in love with a three year old, but I did. It wasn't like falling in love with someone your own age—something I'd only heard about, and had to imagine, like when I borrowed Maddie's teenage magazines, with their love stories.

It was more like finding the perfect toy, or pet. As if it had been made specially for you and only you. I'd never had a special toy—not like Anthony, with his horrible fluffy parrot. Tarik could be my special toy, but be even better, because he was alive, and would love me back.

I'd not seen an Egyptian before—well, half Egyptian, half Devon. He was dressed in a bright yellow T-shirt, which made him look all the darker, silky blue trousers like pyjamas, and lovely little red felt slippers, with neat blue embroidery.

The best bit about him was his little hands and wrists. I liked them because they were fat. The brown skin was a bit loose, allowing him room to grow, I suppose. Somehow, their softness looked OK on him, maybe because his skin was coloured. Not like my arms, all white and dimpled.

'His slippers are from Egypt. His dad sends things sometimes,' said Tina.

'Dad?' said Tarik, looking round hopefully.

'He left when Tarik was only one,' said Tina. 'He can't remember him at all.'

'Dad,' said Tarik again, a bit sadly, I thought. I didn't have a dad either—well, not an active one, only a jailbird. I knew how Tarik felt. But at least he had a mum, and she loved him.

'He's the apple of my eye,' Tina said, as if reading my thoughts. 'Aren't you? The apple of Mummy's eye . . . ' And she picked him up and kissed him all over, ending on his tummy, which made him laugh.

Later, he let me hold him. He sat on my knee and I read him a story book. I could smell him. He smelt like a bar of chocolate.

The apple of his mother's eye. Apples are made to be stolen and eaten, like in the Garden of Eden. It's in the Bible.

Looking back, I suppose it was in that moment that I first decided to steal him and have him for my own. To steal him and have him like in my dream. Stolen fruit always tastes best.

I didn't believe in the Devil. If I had, I could have blamed him, and said he put the thought in my head. No, it was my own thought, and I was going to make it come true.

Three

Black doesn't frighten me. The black cloak that the Dog Whipper wraps round himself wasn't at all scary, nor was the black gloom of the cathedral. I like black.

I often came alone to the cathedral, to get away from the Home. I could be more myself there, and let my imagination go, in the quiet. People didn't seem to think that a girl of twelve, on her own, was anything to get worried about. Sometimes I came at Evensong because I liked the sound of people singing, although I didn't like the words. I came to see the Dog Whipper.

Someone in a science class at school said that black was 'the absence of all colour' and that you get white when all the colours are mixed up. I think it's the other way round. In the black cloak of the Dog Whipper, in the black clothes of the priests, even in the black lettering on the tombs, which I liked to stare at, fascinated about being dead, I saw all the colours of the rainbow.

I'd sit quietly and think about things. Like my name, and my mother, for instance. And that I was ugly and too fat. Blubber is what I called my fat bits—going upwards, my calves, thighs, my big bum, thick waist, the way the flesh at the top of my arms wobbled—and then, my neck wasn't thin enough. My chin was too round, like a pingpong ball, and my cheeks were too soft, like

marshmallows. Only the top of my head had no fat
it, and that's because it was where I kept my brains,
which were my saving grace, as the Christians in this
cathedral would say.

As for my mother, I still wanted to find her, even after
all that she did to me. I thought about her for hours, and
wondered how we could be in touch. I almost prayed for
her, if you want to know the truth.

When I was at the Home, I thought about the cathedral,
rich, mysterious, very old, as if it held the answers to my
problems. When I was at the cathedral, I thought about
the Home, antiseptic, yellow, modern, with no character,
and how to get away from there, but I still hadn't come up
with any easy answers.

The Dog Whipper lived in a little room high above the
nave. He had his own lavatory and tiny kitchen. It said
this in the guide book, which I'd read from cover to cover.
I had never been in his living quarters—he had never
invited me—and I only saw him below, with his wooden
rod and his stern expression.

The guide book said his job in the olden days—from
medieval times right up to only a couple of hundred years
ago—was to chase out the animals from the cathedral
when it was time for a service. In those days, they used to
have meetings and hold markets in the cathedral, which
was the only big covered space in the city, which is a
couple of miles from the Home.

It sounds as if the cathedral was quite fun in those
days. But the crowds got out of control and hadn't come to
worship. That's why they needed a Dog Whipper. I expect
a thousand stray dogs, all mangy and thin, must have felt
his staff on their backs, over the centuries. They'd have
yelped and run for it, out onto the Cathedral Close.

Nowadays there are no dogs or cats or other animals
allowed in the cathedral. There's been a big clean-up. I

...ld have preferred it in the old days. I could ... all the exciting smells and shouting, the candle ... and people selling things, drinking ale from mugs, ...chickens clucking and even goats bleating, everyone ...aring home-made clothes and lots of people with only one eye or bright red boils, or warts with hair growing from them, and beards and beads and everyone with long dirty hair and crutches and funny hats. Then the fierce Dog Whipper appearing and clearing the rabble out, yelling at them and banging his stick. I'd love a job like that. Then people would pay attention to me.

Tonight, at the end of a warm summer's day, the Dog Whipper appeared to me as Evensong was about to begin. Everything was calm. He looked around. No dogs to chase. No cats. No rabble. Only about twenty people, mostly old folk down the front, being respectable. I could see their grey heads in the gloom. I was sitting at the back, in my usual place. I could hear the choirboys coming in from a side entrance. Soon, the singing would start.

The Dog Whipper marched up the aisles, checking all the chapels. No dogs. He looked a bit disappointed, then he relaxed his stern expression. He came to sit beside me, as usual. I was sitting where I could see the murder of Thomas Becket, above me, the silver sword cutting into his skull as he's down on his knees, praying, and I could see the nice coloured carving of the acrobat monk, balancing on his head, and the beautiful angels, fourteen of them, all with their musical instruments high up above. All the things I love.

The Dog Whipper spoke. No one else could see or hear him, I know. It was our special thing. He liked to speak in Italian, because of my name.

'*Ciao*, Bella. *Come stai, carina?*' he said in his teasing but kind voice.

I never reply when he speaks Italian.

'*Non sei venuta ieri sera,*' he said. That means, you didn't come yesterday evening, he translated. He sat down and leant his rod against the seat.

'Can't you see I'm praying?' I said, which wasn't true.

'You? Praying? That'll be the day, you little heathen,' he said. He laughed quietly.

'I didn't come yesterday because they had the inspectors at the Home and I had to stay in,' I said.

'The inspectors?'

'Now and then, they send out people to inspect Children's Homes. I always complain about the food and the staff, and ask to leave, but they never really listen,' I said.

'That is a great shame,' says the Dog Whipper, stroking his chin.

'I wish you could come to visit me there,' I said, but he shook his head. The thing I liked about him was that he always believed my side of things and didn't try to make me change my mind. For instance, he didn't try to make me think I should be grateful for being in the Home, or tell me to fit in better, or anything like that.

'They know I don't want to live there. None of us does. I'd rather be anywhere else in the whole wide world. Can't I come and live here? You could look after me,' I said. We'd been through this before, lots of times.

'That would be impossible,' he said, and sighed. The Dog Whipper sighed a lot, as if he was full of regret. I suppose it was because he was so old, and has seen such a lot of bad things.

He was hundreds of years old, I expect. You couldn't see how old he was, because he looked as if he was only about fifty-five, maybe sixty. He had slightly curly grey hair but it hadn't turned white yet. It reached down to his shoulders, which was very unfashionable, but he didn't care at all about fashion, and laughed at it. 'Vanity, mere vanity,' he would say.

He was all in black, which *is* fashionable. Black boots, with black leggings tucked in them, and a black embroidered shirt with a round neck, and over that his huge black cape which he wrapped around himself, so that you could only see his hands and face. Three white bits in the dark. Like I said, black doesn't scare me.

He had thin, freckly hands, but strong. You could see his knuckles go white when he gripped his rod. His face was quite lined, as if he worried a lot, but not as lined and wrinkled as it would be if it showed his true age. He had lots of hair and eyebrows—big, round, bushy ones. If he looked like his true age, all his hair would have dropped out, long ago, I suppose.

Sometimes he wore a little square black hat with a black tassle hanging from it, but today he didn't. He let me wear it once and I asked if I could have it.

'That would be impossible,' he said, gently, just like he said now. Grown-ups decide too many things are impossible for children.

Like the time I asked the Lady with the Sash—one of the people who show you round the cathedral and tell you all about it—if I could go up the tower.

'Oh, no, dear. We can't let children up there. It's far too dangerous,' she said, adjusting the big red sash across her tummy, and looking down at me.

She was tall, with glasses and a blue perm. She always wore a tartan kilt, with a big silver safety-pin in it. She meant well, I suppose. She always said hello to me since I'd been coming to the cathedral. She didn't know where I came from, and I wasn't going to tell her.

Since I was twelve, they let me go out on my own from the Home. It's a sort of Good Conduct reward, if I get the right number of stars on the wall chart showing my behaviour. I caught the bus from the village where the Home is and came into the city. I usually said I was going shopping. I was allowed out twice a week—big deal—and they said they would make it three times if I didn't get into trouble.

It was part of my training for independence—that's what my Link Worker at the Home called it. Three hours of freedom, twice a week.

The Lady with the Sash saw me coming in tonight. She waved. I ignored her. I found my pew at the back, and she must have thought I was praying. Really, I was waiting for the Dog Whipper.

He sighed again. Just as he did so, the choirboys started singing. The last of the sunlight flooded in through the west window behind me, and for a moment I was covered in green, blue, and red light, which I think made me almost pretty.

I liked it here. I liked the music. In a moment, maybe the big organ would start up. I liked the tombs, all decorated. I liked the ones which have got graffiti on them, best. It shows that vandals were around long ago, not just nowadays. One person scratched his name in 1642.

I liked the carvings on the old oak benches—animals, birds, angels. You could rub them with your fingers, like children have for hundreds of years. They're all smoothed from centuries of children doing it. I liked all the angels, knights, bishops, who all talked to me. Some people would call them ghosts. I liked the mystery.

Most of all, I liked the Dog Whipper. He was my friend. He was probably my best friend, if you really want to know.

Four

Instead of stealing Tarik from Tina straightaway, I ran away from the Home.

Maddie dared me to do it. It was like she was testing me, because I challenged her being the boss of the Big Three.

'This is useless. We haven't done anything yet,' I'd said after getting back from the cathedral one afternoon. 'You're meant to be the boss. Lead us, then.'

'I'm still thinking . . . planning things,' she lied. We'd thought of things like going out at night and trying to get hold of some drink. But nothing came of it.

So I had another go at her, which was a bad idea. She challenged me to run away. 'To prove you're not all mouth.'

I'd run away once before, but only for two hours, and in the daytime. They found me on the farm next door, in the haystack.

'This time, you've got to run away all night, in the town,' she said, with a hard edge to her voice.

'And if I do?'

'Well, then I'll listen to what you want the Big Three to do. We can do whatever you say,' she said.

'Is that a promise?'

'On my mother's life,' she said, which was a joke,

because she didn't have a mother. Her mother was dead. Topped herself.

So, I said I'd do it.

It was one of the days I was allowed to go into the town, so I knew no one would miss me. Not until it got dark, at about seven.

I took some extra tuna sandwiches and two packets of stolen biscuits. I knew I'd be hungry. I said goodbye to Maddie and Anthony.

I went to the cathedral. The Lady with the Sash was hovering around the entrance, where they ask you to make a donation to keep the cathedral going, which I never do because I'm always skint, and she said hello. I know she wanted to be kind, but I didn't want to talk to her. She had a big, high, calm forehead but she kind of frowned with her mouth, looking at me doubtfully. She didn't know what to make of me, but was interested. Best to avoid her. I thought she might guess I'd run away. I walked down the nave.

I could hear the wind whistling high up in the vaults, every time the big doors to the cathedral opened. I could smell the damp old stone, and the lavender polish, from the wooden pews. Also, there was a smell from the candles in one of the chapels, and there were some lilies, in a big flower arrangement, and their scent nearly made me faint. I could hear the big gold clock, with its pictures of the sun and moon and stars, chime when it got to be four o'clock. At the same time, high up outside, I could hear the bell in the tower strike. Now and then you'd hear someone muttering a prayer in one of the side chapels.

I had a certain routine to bring me luck. It meant I had to touch the tombs in a special order, including two bishops, who had to have their noses stroked, and a little stone dog who lay beneath a knight's feet. He had to have his ears scratched. The dog, I mean, not the knight.

A man was moving chairs around for a concert in the evening. They scraped on the stone floor. People were walking up and down, peering at the tombs and the statues. They were all talking to each other in that church whispery voice people put on, as if God might overhear them.

I found one of the little wooden mirror carts they have here—it's like a pram, but with a mirror on it, facing upwards, so that you can look at the ceiling without cricking your neck. I pushed it along, making a squeaking, creaking noise, looking at the gold, red, and blue carved and painted bits.

I was waiting for the Dog Whipper. He always knew when I was in the cathedral.

I was sitting down near the choir, looking up at the limestone carving of the mother sow suckling her piglets. Pigs are my favourite animals, because they are so intelligent. I liked this little carving, because it was so simple, just made of stone, not decorated, and because it made me think how nice it would be to be close to your mum. When I looked up at her, the mother pig grunted, in a sort of satisfied way, looked down and blinked. She shifted her place, on the ceiling, but the piglets didn't like this, and began to squeal. Then the Dog Whipper appeared, from nowhere, like he does.

'*Ciao*, Bella,' he said, but I wasn't falling for any of that Italian stuff.

'I see there's a concert here this evening,' I said.

'Yes. It's Mozart, my favourite,' he said.

I hated classical music, and said so.

He sighed. 'Sometimes, you disappoint me, Bella,' he said.

I didn't like this. 'I thought we were friends,' I said.

'So we are.'

'Well, you shouldn't criticize me, just because I don't like the same kind of crappy music that you do.'

24

He went a bit pink. I know he didn't like me swearing. It probably reminded him of the rabble swearing at him when he used to clear them out of the cathedral, hundreds of years ago.

The Dog Whipper has got a white flattened tip to his nose, as if he has it pressed up all the while against an invisible pane of glass. He looked funny, with this white tip and the rest of his face pink, just because I had sworn a little bit. I knew lots of worse words. I laughed.

'Rudolph the white-nosed reindeer,' I said, pointing at him. He didn't understand, and I had to explain about Santa and his reindeer at Christmas, and sing him a bit of the song. He sighed again, and I could tell I had disappointed him again. He didn't think much of the modern Christmas, with all its presents and eating too much. I think he preferred the idea of starving himself, or even whipping himself. I'd read that that is what they used to do, in medieval times, to get closer to God. Very strange.

He changed the subject, and asked me how things were at the Children's Home.

'Fine,' I said in a high I-don't-care-a-damn voice. I wasn't going to tell him I'd run away. I had an idea beginning to form. I'd come back when it was getting dark and pretend to go to the concert. Then I'd find somewhere to hide and I'd stay the night in the cathedral. I felt at home here.

I walked around the town by myself. The town centre, which was bombed in the War, is ugly and 1950s and there are hardly any of the old black and white buildings left. The cathedral was bombed, too, but luckily the church men had taken the best bits away—like the east window, for example—and put them into storage. The Dog

Whipper told me about this. He likes to go on about history.

I walked past the usual shops—Waterstone's book shop, McDonald's, which made me feel hungry, Boots. Then I turned right, down past the bus station and across a roundabout. I said hello to several of the street people as I went. I quite liked the beggars, and their dogs. Sometimes I thought the Dog Whipper wouldn't like them, though.

Then I walked across a big car park and at the bottom, across the road, near a pub, there was some waste ground, behind a rusty fence. I stood by the gate and stared in, making sure there weren't any murderers lurking.

I think about death a lot. Which isn't surprising, seeing that my mother would pretend to be dying so often. I wondered what it would be like, to be dead and in your grave, or to be just a handful of grey dust, like my nan, in an urn on the shelf. Once, when I was about nine, quite soon after she died, I had been alone in the house. I took a deep breath and told myself not to be afraid. I took the top off the urn, and tipped some of the dust onto my hand, and felt it there, dry and light, and even sniffed it, but it didn't smell of my nan. It smelt of nothing at all. I wondered if there was someone else's dust, too, mixed in with Nan.

How did they sieve it out and make sure it didn't get mixed up, and break the bones into small bits and then make it into dust? I wanted to know all about it. I wanted to visit a crematorium and have a guided tour to find out, but of course when I said this to my social worker she nearly had a fit and I had to say I was only joking. Which I wasn't.

I'd never been to a funeral—my mum wouldn't let me go to Nan's—and I wanted to know all about what happened. But my mother wouldn't talk about it at all and always changed the subject.

I sat down on a fallen tree trunk, and started eating my tuna sandwiches with mayonnaise, and a whole packet of biscuits, washed down with a can of cola. If anyone came up to me, I'd planned my escape route. I'd be straight across to the pub, screaming. But no one paid any attention to me, which was a bit disappointing, in a way.

Then I walked back the way I had come, but turned right and went down by the station and across the big river, which comes down from the moor to the north and goes out to sea a few miles south of here. I was getting a bit tired, and stopped to watch the trains. I ate the last of my sandwiches and wondered where my mum was. The trains were running alongside the river, clanking and looking all bright and warm. I wanted to be on one.

They were going north, maybe to Yorkshire, where she was locked up. I'd never been to Yorkshire. I tried to imagine it, but all I could think of was *Wuthering Heights* because it's set in Yorkshire, and then I got the song by Kate Bush in my head, and that put me in a bad mood. I hate Kate Bush. She sounds like a hippy being strangled.

Then I walked back to the cathedral, eating the second packet of biscuits. My legs were aching by now, and I was glad to sit down.

I got in by pretending to be with a large group of people who had tickets. The person on the door, one of the old dodderers with sashes, didn't count them.

I sat down in my favourite place near the font. The concert was about to begin.

Five

The music was cool. I had to admit it. I'd never heard a big choir before, or an orchestra. It was Mozart's *Requiem*, all about the death of Christ, and I'm addicted to things about death. I was carried away and nearly cried, which wasn't like me, because I was hard.

I didn't know anything about Mozart. I wanted to ask the Dog Whipper about him. But the Dog Whipper hadn't shown up. It's always that he has to find me, not the other way round. I never know where he is. Maybe he was watching the crowd, from his place over the nave, in case there were any hooligan elements, although a riot didn't seem likely. They were all well-behaved, clapped in the right places, clapped at the end and someone gave bouquets to the soloists and then everyone trooped out, leaving lots of money to be counted to keep the cathedral going. Everybody happy, I suppose.

I'd spotted where to hide, when I came earlier. There are always repairs going on in the cathedral and in one corner, near the big clock, some scaffolding was stacked, with a tarpaulin over it. I crawled under it and sat with my back to the cold stone wall until I could no longer hear anyone moving about. I heard the key click in the big double door, with an echo. I was all alone in the cathedral.

I looked up, and smelt the oldness. The damp stone. How did the masons make stone so feathery, though? The vaults and ribs all fan out and it's like a big bird is up there, protecting you with its feathery wings. Or maybe it's a protecting angel. Maybe you are meant to think of angels. I liked the idea of something protecting me. I curled up and fell asleep for a bit.

But I hadn't thought about the cold. It was still September, with summer hardly over, but the floor was as cold as ice. I went to sit in one of the chapels, where there's a nice thick carpet, but it was still cold.

Where was the Dog Whipper? He'd be able to help me.

But it seemed as if he was having a night off. I walked around, trying to keep warm. It must have been about midnight by now. The clock had struck eleven a long time ago.

I looked up to the east window. Moonlight was coming in, shining through it. I knew the window well. It's my favourite, with its lovely green, red, purple, and blue glass held together by lead. It's very old. Eight hundred years old, I think.

Then a strange thing happened. I was looking at Saint Sidwell, up on the left-hand side, with her little golden scythe in her hand and her gold hair glowing in the moonlight, and I was thinking how beautiful and slim and pretty she was, not like me at all.

Then she began to move.

It happened like this. It was like a transfer peeling off—one of those ones you can stick on your arm, but have to put in water first, until it gets loose.

First, her feet peeled off from the glass, then her long purple dress, all its segments, then her gold buttons one by one and her hand and then her neck and head in pure white glass and then she was floating in front of the

29

window, high there up above my head, and then she just slowly, so slowly, floated down, feet first, and landed silently in the choir in front of me.

She was one dimensional, thinner than paper. When she turned sideways for a moment, she disappeared completely. She was a thin transfer, only visible from the front. Maybe that's the way ghosts work. Maybe only people who are standing directly in front of them can see them.

I didn't know what to say at first. I knew about Saint Sidwell. Anyone does, who lives around here. They taught me in school. How she was a very early Christian saint, and her story.

How she was engaged to be married to a local yokel and how his mother took against her and told the other peasants out in the field to murder her. How they cut her throat with her own scythe. How a holy spring flooded out of the ground, where she fell dying.

Yes, everyone knows about Saint Sidwell, around here. But no one had spoken to her before. I still didn't know what to say.

She seemed to know me. 'You have had misfortune, as I have. Am I right?' she said. Her voice was very gentle. I nodded.

It was dark and I couldn't see very well but she was holding her throat and when she took her hand away I could see the jagged, thin scar, a foot long and at an angle, so that it started under one ear, her left one, and ended at the breastbone on her right side. The scar was not white, like the rest of her complexion, but a livid pink. It looked recent. Raised up from the rest of her skin. She saw me staring at it, and put her hand back.

She was so beautiful, with her golden hair and her slim white hands with long fingers and fine fingernails. Her little pink mouth and big, sad eyes. Yet she was embarrassed, because I had spotted her hurt place, her ugly place.

I was looking at her ugly place, but I was ugly all over. Or that was how I felt, and she seemed to know.

'We have both known misfortune. Yet we are very different,' she said, taking a little step forwards. She was not much older than me, fifteen, sixteen, maybe. At last I could speak.

'Different time, different families, different stories . . . ' I babbled. I just had to say something, and didn't make much sense.

'Ah. Families,' she said. 'You do not have a family, I can sense.'

I thought the Dog Whipper must have been telling her about me. I'd spilled most of my story to him, over the past few weeks, since I started coming to the cathedral.

'Did the Dog Whipper tell you? Where's he got to, tonight?'

'No, he told me almost nothing about you. He just said that there would be a girl alone in the cathedral tonight, and that I might like to talk to you, when midnight came.'

Just as she said this, I heard the clock begin to strike.

'You were early,' I said.

'Only by a minute,' she said and laughed. She had a lovely laugh. It was golden, if you can imagine that. Golden like her hair and her scythe, which I now noticed she was still carrying, in her left hand. It was very old-fashioned but it glinted sharp in the crack of moonlight which came in from a high window, when a cloud blew away.

I decided to tell her everything, and it all came bursting out. After a while, she put her hand on my arm and gently stopped me.

'Should you not be at home, my dear? It's very late,' she said. It sounded funny, being called 'my dear' by someone who looked only a few years older than me. Then I thought that, really, she was hundreds of years older. Maybe that was the way they spoke, then.

'I've run away. From the Children's Home,' I said, and then I had to explain what a Children's Home was.

'It's a place where they pay people to come and look after you while you are growing up because your parents are dead or can't cope with you and no one else can cope with you either, not the foster carers or the people who might want to adopt you.'

Then she wanted to know what sort of things I had done to make people not cope with me and I ran through the list.

'Steal. Lie. Get angry. Smash things up, sometimes. Be too noisy. Break their rules. Be too anxious and make them anxious. Keep testing them out to see if they love me—you know, just wanting too much and when you don't get it turning nasty and always be on their case and wanting to know everything that is going on and not letting them have their privacy . . . '

'And it worked. You proved they couldn't manage you,' she said.

By this time we were sitting down side by side on a pew. Suddenly I thought this must be what it would be like to have an older sister who cared about you. I'd never had a sister, or a brother.

'Did you ever have a sister?' I asked.

'Oh, yes, a great many. Both brothers and sisters. In my day, families were very large . . . although a lot died very young, and at birth,' she said. I began to think that nowadays, at least, we had medicine and good food and warm clothes.

Thinking of warm clothes made me shiver, and she noticed.

'I will be back,' she said.

I was alone again. I looked up to where the fourteen angels were playing their medieval instruments, silently. Bagpipes, horns, flutes, stringed instruments. Each angel had more or less the same coloured wings, a sort of pearly grey, but their clothes were of different colours, long flowing robes. You could see their little feet. I was thinking how cold their feet must be when Saint Sidwell came back. She had three lovely fleecy blankets. She didn't say where she had found them.

I put one under me, on the thick carpet, and two over me. I was feeling very tired, and wanted to talk to Saint Sidwell some more, but felt my eyelids closing.

The last thing I remember, she was singing me a lullaby.

'It is the one my mother used to sing to me,' she said. I didn't understand the words of the song. They were in a strange language, with lots of throaty noises in it, like gentle coughing, and they sent me to sleep.

The next thing I knew it was morning, with sun streaming in the east window, Saint Sidwell back in her place up there, frozen in stained glass, and I was being woken up angrily by one of the vergers who had opened the cathedral.

Then it was a day of question time, the police, Social Services, the usual story.

Back to the Children's Home, and trouble. But I had stayed away for the night, and Maddie looked at me with some kind of respect when the policewoman brought me in. She was three years older than me, but she respected me. It felt good. I wished I had had an older sister.

Back to the Home. Same old food, same old routine. But I felt different, now. Sort of older and wiser. But I felt a bit more desperate, too, to be honest.

Six

I suppose you could say this was the beginning of my mad period. Loony Toon time. The time when I went off my head good and proper.

They grounded me at the Home. No more trips to town. They said I had broken trust, let the side down, by not keeping to the bargain we had struck. Whose side, I wanted to know?

So, apart from going to school, I was stuck in one place. No more going to the cathedral. No more talks with the Dog Whipper. I missed him; but the trouble was, I couldn't tell anyone. Not even Maddie, who was being quite friendly now that I had run away. No one would believe me about the Dog Whipper, Saint Sidwell, and the other things. As each day went by, I began to not believe it myself.

'Could you do me a favour?' I asked Maddie one Saturday. She was about to go into town to get her hair cut, yet again. She had been boring me with the details of what style she wanted, and what her non-existent boyfriend would have to say about it.

'Yup,' she said, combing her hair, then doing her eye make-up. We were in one of the bathrooms, and none of the staff had spotted we were together, for the moment. They soon would, though.

'Can you deliver a letter for me?'

'Where to?'

'To the cathedral.'

'The cathedral?' She looked at me hard, as if I were crazy. Which I was, of course.

'Who's it for?'

'Someone. I can't tell you.'

Of course, that got her asking more questions, but I didn't budge.

'All you've got to do is put it somewhere. I'll tell you. You don't have to speak to anyone, or anything.'

'Oh, OK then,' she said, when she realized she wasn't going to get any information out of me, 'but write it quick. I'm going in ten minutes.'

I went back to my room. I was worried about Maddie taking the letter. It was for the Dog Whipper, but I knew she would try to read it. What could I say?

Then I thought that I didn't even know his name.

Dear DW, I wrote on some blue paper with little pigs on it. I only used his initials so that Maddie wouldn't know who I was writing to. *It's ages since I saw you. More than two weeks. I'm not allowed to come into town any more, since they found me in the cathedral. My friend Maddie is delivering this letter. All I want to say is that I am still a prisoner here. It's worse than ever, now that I'm not allowed to go out. No one understands me, except maybe you. Please can you write to me? Tell me what to do. I don't know when I will be allowed into town again. With love, Bella.*

I put it in a plain envelope, wrote DW in big letters on the front, and told Maddie to put it under the door leading to his little set of rooms on the north side of the nave— the rooms I'd never been allowed to visit.

Later that evening Maddie came back. All she wanted to talk about was her new hairstyle—shorter, sleeker, which made her look even prettier and so I liked her even less. She kept combing it, back-combing it, spraying on stuff to make it spikier, and saying how her boyfriend couldn't keep his hands off it. Which none of us believed.

We were all having supper together. It was Anthony's favourite, burgers and chips, and he ate double portions. The little kids teased him because he was getting whiter and fatter than ever. 'Mr Blobby', one of them kept calling him. There was nearly a fight when Anthony suddenly smacked him in the face, and someone threw tomato sauce across the room. Then the staff started shouting at us and making their usual threats about not allowing us computer games, taking away the TV, no more outings. The usual adult blackmail rubbish.

The woman staff member with the wispy blonde moustache, dangly green ear-rings, nose stud, dungarees, and with a voice like sandpaper tried to make us all sit with our hands on our lips, to keep quiet, but Anthony blew a loud raspberry, which made the little ones laugh and that made the staff scream at us some more.

Then Maddie had to make it even worse.

'Bella's got a boyfriend, Bella's got a boyfriend,' she started chanting. She had turned on me, and I thought we were friends. I denied it, and could feel myself getting red in the face.

'Bella's got a boyfriend. He's called DW. Is it David? Danny? Duncan? She sends him love letters. On piggy notepaper. Sealed with a loving kiss,' she shouted. All the other kids wanted to know what she was talking about. I grabbed her and pulled her hair, which was not so short that I couldn't get a good handful. She screamed.

I love a good ruck. I'm a natural fighter, bigger and heavier than Maddie. A bruiser, is what my dad used to call me. I love it when you get a good handful of hair, and twist as hard as you can, or when a punch goes in just where you aimed it. A kick in the guts is good too, or a good wrestling hold, when you could break an arm if you wanted to. Skin twisting. Bruises coming. I've often wondered what it would be like, to hear a bone break. Would it just be a dull little click, like when you are in the woods and tread on a stick?

I love it when the person you're fighting screams, or asks for mercy. Some don't, until you make them. Me, I never ask for mercy. I bite my lip and take the pain.

So then the staff had to separate us and put us in our rooms early for the night and all that usual rubbish. At least I had stopped Maddie from talking about my letter.

Next day, she was back on speaking terms. These things pass over quickly in the Home. We've only got each other, really, me and Maddie, and sometimes Anthony.

She even apologized.

'But what made you make that up?' I asked.

'Because I thought you did have a boyfriend. That DW person, whoever he is. The one I delivered the letter to.'

'He's not my boyfriend. So you did deliver it, then?'

'Yes, I did. I slid it under the door you told me to. What's it all about, Bella?'

'None of your business. And you haven't answered my question. You had no right to tell everyone about my letter.'

'I didn't tell everyone. You didn't give me a chance. When you grabbed my hair, it really hurt.'

'Good! It was meant to hurt. I had to do something. But I bet I know why you made up a story about me having a boyfriend.'

'Why?'

'It's because you were jealous. You thought I had a boyfriend and you don't have one, do you?'

She didn't say anything.

'Do you?'

'I did have one, a real one, but only for a week. He dumped me.'

'When?'

'Back in the summer holidays.'

'Ages ago, and you've been lying ever since.'

'So?'

I stopped. It was no good going on at her. Everyone wants to be loved. I said I wouldn't tell anyone about her lies, if she wouldn't tell anyone about my letter. It was a deal.

So then, I waited for a letter back. But none came. I waited three whole weeks. I began to think that I had imagined the whole thing, and that frightened me. Maybe I was mad, like my mother. I tried drawing the Dog Whipper and Saint Sidwell, just to remind me how they looked, but I couldn't get it right.

All I could draw properly was the Lady with the Sash, and she was a real person, all too ordinary, and I wasn't interested in her. It made me so cross. I could copy exactly her little bluey-grey curls and the tartan of her skirt with its big silver pin and her pearl necklace and the big red sash, and all I wanted to draw, but couldn't, was the deep black of the Dog Whipper's hood, his kind, twinkly eyes looking out from under it, the funny white tip to his nose, and the purple robes and golden curls of Saint Sidwell, the nice golden buttons of her bodice.

I ripped up the drawings and set fire to them with some matches in the garden, and that got me into more trouble, especially when I wouldn't tell any of the staff why I was doing it.

'Your behaviour is becoming more and more disturbed,' my Link Worker said. 'How would you like to see a counsellor?' I just grunted like one of my favourite pigs and looked at the floor and decided not to speak.

I kept it up for two days. I didn't say a word. So then they got in the child psychiatrist—a man with big brown-framed glasses and a jacket with patches on the elbows.

At least it was one-to-one attention, although not the same as the Dog Whipper.

We got round to what I really wanted, most of all. What would I like, if anything were possible, he asked, sitting across the desk in the play therapy room they have at the Home. Up to that point, I hadn't said a word.

'To see my mum!' I shouted in the biggest voice I could make, and he jumped, and dropped his pen. 'To see my mum, you idiot, like I've always wanted to.'

'But that would . . . not be appropriate,' he said, picking up his pen and arranging his papers on the desk. 'You are In Care. The Council has to act in your best interests, Bella, as if it were your parent, and it is not best for you at the moment to see your mother. The courts have said so.'

'Where is she?' I asked. 'It's somewhere in Yorkshire, isn't it? She's locked up, somewhere in Yorkshire. It's on my file, but it doesn't say where.'

'She is in Yorkshire, yes. She is not at all well. Perhaps, if she gets better, a visit could be arranged. You must be patient. To see her now would not be . . . appropriate.' I hated the word appropriate. It was a grown-up word, meaning they knew best.

I swore at him then, some new words I had learned from the foul-mouthed youngest resident of the Home, little rat-face, a whole stream of them, one after the other. He blinked and adjusted his glasses, and wrote something down on the pad in front of him. I walked out and he didn't try to stop me.

Seven

The Dog Whipper never wrote to me. I suppose if he had, it would have risked other people finding out about him. Instead, he visited me when I was asleep. I mean that he came in a dream, but it seemed more real than so-called real life.

In the dream, I was in a TV quiz show. The spotlight was on me. I had got through the previous rounds and now it was my solo turn, for the big money. The quizmaster came up close and I could smell his horrible aftershave, so strong it made me want to puke, and see that his front top teeth were false—which you can't see at home on the telly—and he was giving me the big 'Aren't you a brave girl and so clever to have come so far?' routine. The audience was out there somewhere in the dark and I couldn't see them against the bright lights. Me, nervous? No. I'm never nervous. Just hard.

Then there was the loud music and the ticking clock and the questions began.

They were so difficult! I had to pass on the first three and was just beginning to want to give up when the Dog Whipper came to my side—except that, as usual, no one could see him. He began to whisper the answers in my ear.

'When was the Battle of Hastings?' We never did that at school, and I hadn't a clue, but the Dog Whipper whispered, '1066. The Norman Conquest, when they came to conquer England. They were a little bit before my time, but they built wonderful cathedrals . . . ' and so I said in a big voice, '1066.'

'Which Pope succeeded John the Twenty-Third?' and, of course, I hadn't a clue again, not being religious, but the Dog Whipper said, 'Paul the Sixth. Rather a reactionary, I'm afraid . . . ' and he carried on into my ear but I shouted out 'Paul the Sixth' and doubled my money, and the audience cheered me.

'Which of the Spice Girls first released a solo record?' was the next question and of course I knew the answer to that, but had to put up with the Dog Whipper asking me really stupid things like, 'Who are the Spice Girls? What is a solo record, please?' and I flapped at him with my hand, and put my finger to my fat little lips to tell him to keep quiet, which must have looked pretty strange on TV. Not just fat, but shooing something invisible, her imaginary friend, away.

Just then the quizmaster said time was up and I'd have to come back next week. He put his horrible over-friendly arm round me, saying, 'Give a big hand to little Bella,' and the audience was cheering. I hated it when he called me little, because he meant big. Too big. Anyone could see that. They should have put a special shrinking lens on the telly camera when it pointed at me, I was thinking. Then the spotlight went off, but the dream didn't finish.

In the next scene I was in the changing room, eating a triple-decker tuna sandwich, drinking a banana milkshake and taking off all the TV make-up. The Dog Whipper was watching and he kept saying, 'Extraordinary, quite extraordinary! Do you say that twenty million people watch this rubbish?' but I threw a wet flannel at him and he shut up.

Now that we were alone together I could ask him what I should do about my life and he asked me the same question as the psychiatrist had done. 'What do you most want?' and I said again, 'To see my mum,' but I didn't shout it out this time.

'Then that is what you must do . . . see her,' he began.

'But I don't know where she is! No one will tell me. It's a state secret, or something. It's in Yorkshire, somewhere, in a special place for people who are ill. She's locked up, and I don't know where to find her.'

'Ah, I see,' he said, stroking his chin. 'I will have to make some enquiries for you.'

I looked at him. Something was different. In the cathedral, he has his big stick, which he calls his staff, with him, usually in his right hand. He doesn't actually carry a whip—at least, I've never seen him with one.

But today he had no whip, no stick, nothing. His cloak was brown, shorter, not black. His hair was tied back, off his face. It made him seem less fierce, and I asked him about it.

'Oh, that's simple. When I am out of the cathedral, I am off-duty, as you would say. I don't need a stick. It would only worry people.'

'And your cloak, your long grey hair and face don't scare people, I suppose?' I said, teasing him. He looked puzzled.

'Haven't you ever thought you might look a bit frightening, to some people? Not me, I'm not frightened of anything, but little children might be,' I said.

'Most people cannot see me,' he said.

'Could the people in the audience see you, tonight?'

He laughed. 'Oh, no. Not them. They wanted to believe something else . . . to believe in the picture painted for them of brave little Bella, all alone. The only people who can see me are those who need to. Special people . . . '

'You mean, others *can* see you . . . not just me?' I couldn't believe it.

'Oh, no, Bella, not just you,' he said, and I felt very disappointed.

Then, just as I was going to ask him more, the dream faded away.

I woke, all stressed out. I'd overslept. I saw Tina Bloor at the end of my bed, with all her cleaning stuff in her little trolley. The vacuum cleaner, the dustpans, brushes, cloths, the polish which smelt like lavender.

'I was having a dream,' I said.

'That's nice, Bella,' she said. 'Like the first time I met you. Dreams are important. And horoscopes.'

'My friend was in it,' I said, still sleepy, but not so sleepy that I was going to tell her his name.

'That's nice,' she said, in her soft west-country voice. 'But I've got to do your room, now. Is that all right, my love?' She was such a softie, so nice. I wanted her to have a better job than just being a cleaner. I wanted her to stand up for herself. She made me cross.

It was autumn half-term, which was why I was still in bed late. Then I noticed something. She'd brought Tarik with her. He was out in the corridor, but putting his head round the door, giving me a shy smile.

'Tarik!' I said, sitting up in bed and holding out my hands and he ran in and gave me a cuddle, which Tina didn't seem to mind. I was so glad he remembered me from the time I had been to his house.

He had on the same lovely little red felt slippers with blue embroidery and his dark hair had been sloshed with water and combed carefully sideways. He smelt of chocolate, like before, and I squeezed him.

'Why are you here today?' I said. He had never been to the Home before.

'Nursery closed,' he said. He began to pat my hand with his, which was soft and brown and warm. 'No nursery today. I came with Mummy.'

'It's because of half-term they're closed,' said Tina. 'Now, excuse me for asking, but are you going to get up or shall I do your room later?'

'I'll get up now that Tarik's here. Can I play with him?' I asked, and she said yes. Tina was too nice. She made me suspicious, the way she always seemed to want to please me.

I jumped out of bed while they waited outside, and got dressed. I went through the dream about the Dog Whipper again. He was going to help me, he said. He was going to get some advice. I wondered how long he would be, and whether I would dream of him again the next night.

Then I played with Tarik for a whole hour. I made sure none of the other kids in the Home saw me. Playing with three year olds is not what your average hard girl does, much. We played boats in the little stream which ran at the bottom of the big garden. The best thing about the Home was the garden, which had big oak trees, swings and places to hide under bushes, and the nicest, cleanest little stream where there were sometimes ducks, quite tame ones you could feed, and where you could launch boats and have races.

There were some bulrushes growing at one end of the stream, big brown ones. I saw a kingfisher there, like an electric streak. There was watercress growing on the banks, and small yellow pebbles under the clear water. The stream was just made for stick and boat races.

This was an old game for the kids at the Home, but Tarik had never played it before. He jumped up and down and even though he was only three he wanted to win, and I let him. I made sure not to take him to the branch of the stream which was muddy, full of frogspawn in the spring and sometimes sticklebacks. There were nettles growing around it, as if to keep you out. It smelt rich and swampy, and when you took your shoes off the mud oozed smoothly through your toes, like thick black cream, and we used to pretend there were crocodiles there. I didn't want to frighten Tarik. It was a place for older children.

His boat, which I'd made out of an empty cola bottle and cardboard, which I taped on to make a sail, was called Pharaoh—because Tarik was half Egyptian—and mine was called Demolisher, because I wrapped bits of black bin bag round it and stuck some nails in it, pointing outwards, to sink Pharaoh with.

I let him win three races and he was skipping up and down the bank squealing with excitement and then he fell in, but not deep, and cried.

I thought Tina would be angry with me for letting him get wet but she wasn't. She'd seen what happened by watching us through a window—someone is always watching you in the Home—and knew the water wasn't deep.

The best thing was that Tarik didn't blame me. This showed that he trusted me, I thought. He sat on my knee after Tina had taken off some of his wet clothes. Having him sitting there, smiling while I talked to him, made me want a baby of my own so much that it hurt my heart, a stabbing pain like when you get indigestion.

I was too young to have one and anyway I thought I'd never get a boyfriend, because I was too fat. But I thought I could borrow Tarik. That's the only way I can explain how I felt. I thought it would be lovely to have someone love me and want me, all the while. That's why I was determined to take Tarik with me, next time I ran away.

Eight

The trouble was, I was being watched by the staff too closely to make another break for it. I had to be patient, and not get caught out when being wicked. I sat in my room, and planned things.

One day, after autumn half-term, Maddie and Anthony were standing upstairs in the corridor, near one of the bathrooms. It was the hour before bed, when we liked to wind up the staff.

Anthony suggested we set off the fire alarms. He liked to see the staff panic, and the fire engines come racing into the courtyard of the Home from the fire station, nearly three miles away. He kept a book of how long it took them. The record was seven minutes, and Anthony thought that was too slow.

'They should be able to do it in five minutes. I'm going to write to my MP to complain,' he said. He could be very pompous at times.

'No, you'll only get into trouble. The staff know it's you. It's always you,' I said.

'How about flooding the bathrooms—like we did before, and the water ran all downstairs when we put cotton wool in the overflow holes?' said Maddie, without sounding very interested.

'No. That's an old one,' I said.

'Well, what can you think of doing that's new?' Anthony asked.

'I thought we were going to do something different. We had that idea of calling ourselves the Big Bad Three, weeks ago. I thought we were going to be a gang and do things down town . . . ' I said.

'Yes, we were, until you were grounded,' Maddie said, picking at a fingernail and looking bored.

'Well, I'll think of something for when they let me out again,' I said. 'Something down town, where no one will know us.' Then a member of staff—one of the women with bristles—poked her head into the corridor with its horrible washable yellow walls, all shiny, and stared at us.

'What are you three plotting?' she said.

'World War Three,' we said, all together. As if we were going to tell her.

A week later, I had an interview with my Link Worker. She sat me down in the office and we had this big heart-to-heart about my behaviour. For the past fortnight—since the incident with my little bonfire in the garden—I hadn't been caught doing anything naughty. She told me they were going to relax the rules and let me go into town, just the once.

I pretended to be very grateful.

'But not by yourself. You can't be trusted not to run away again, yet, Bella. You have to go with Anthony and Maddie. Just for a Saturday afternoon. Two hours, maximum. They'll keep an eye on you.'

Great, I thought. *Foolish Link Worker*. It was time to think up something for the Big Bad Three to do. Their first evil act. It's surprising what can be achieved if you plan ahead. Anthony said we ought to do something about what he called the Consumer Society.

'All those people just earning and then spending. Greedy pigs,' he said.

'Don't be horrible about pigs,' I said, and punched him in his stomach, which was, I must admit, a large target.

'Sorry, Bella,' he said. He remembered that I thought pigs were the best animals in the world. 'But it's true. We live in a very materialistic world, you know. All that consumption makes it harder for people like us, who don't have any money. Or only pocket-money.'

I said I would try to think of something. Then, later, I began to think about the big supermarket in the town, one of the biggest in the country, with its twenty checkouts, twenty-four-hour opening, thousands of customers obeying the command to spend, spend, spend. I hated it, with its sing-song customer service announcements, chanted to us like we were all stupid, and its shop girls in their naff nylon uniforms. I felt a bit sorry for them. I was never, ever going to be a shop girl. Yes, the supermarket would be a good place to start our Big Three exploits. But who would be our first victim?

It was Tina Bloor. She was too kind and nice, so had to be punished. She had to take to her bed for a day afterwards to recover.

We knew her movements, which were routine as clockwork. On Saturdays she would do her supermarket shopping.

Maddie had an older friend, called Veronique, who was in all the drama productions at their school. She loved acting and had lessons and wanted to go on the stage. We persuaded her to join us at the supermarket and told her what to do.

Tina came into view, hurrying as usual and talking to

herself. 'Cat meat, dog meat, meat and mincemeat. Mincemeat, raisins, suet, cat food, dog meat, meat,' she was saying as she stepped inside. She was planning to make a Christmas pudding.

'What did my boy Tony say not to forget? Oh yes. He likes them new oven chips. The crispy, spicy ones. I mustn't forget them, or he'll be cross.' She let Tony rule her life. Doormat was Tina's middle name. *Walk all over me.*

'Congratulations, madam,' Veronique said, stepping forward and putting on a cracked grown-up voice. She was wearing glasses, platform shoes, and looked about eighteen. She'd borrowed a store uniform from someone who worked there.

Tina, who was very short-sighted, jumped about a foot. She squinted at Veronique. 'What have I done?' she asked in her piping voice, as if she were accused of something. She didn't know Veronique.

'You are our one hundred-thousandth customer,' Veronique boomed.

'Oh,' said Tina. 'Ooh. That's very nice, my love.'

'And you've just won a three minute trolley dash through the supermarket,' Veronique said. 'You can keep everything you can collect in three minutes.'

'Oh,' said Tina, playing for time. 'That's very nice.' Then it sank in. You could tell, because she turned the colour of the bright pink balloons telling shoppers to buy early for Christmas. Her hands started wringing each other, like she was trying to squeeze water out.

'Er, excuse me for asking, like, but when do I do it?' she said.

'Right now, madam.'

'Now?' squeaked Tina. 'But I haven't got time to ask Tone what he wants me to get him!' Her little hands had gone to her throat in panic.

'I'm afraid so. Publicity deadline. Now, we're going to count down to zero and away you go. There'll be someone at the other end to take down the details . . . and we'll be providing special transport home, in a Rolls Royce, for all those goodies you're about to collect! Thirty seconds, twenty-nine, twenty-eight . . . ' Veronique said.

Anthony, Maddie, and I, hiding in the cereals section, and all wearing dark glasses to disguise us, clutched each other as Tina, who's usually so mild, went sort of wild-eyed, seized a trolley, and positioned herself at the start formed by the chrome turnstile. She looked like the shopper from hell.

'Five, four, three, two, one, go! Off you go, Mrs Bloor. Good luck!' Veronique gave the turnstiles a good shove and Tina shot through like a greyhound out of a trap. The store was quite crowded. Even though she was small, Tina moved quickly. She was through the starting blocks and into fruit and veg within three seconds.

'Pineapples, they'll keep. Ooh, grapes at one pound fifty a pound. I can't afford those. Ooh, no, I can, it's free.' She grabbed two huge bunches of grapes, threw them to the bottom of the shopping trolley then threw them out again because she must have thought they'd get crushed. This dithering took her twenty seconds.

'Ooh. What would Tone want? I wish he was here,' she squeaked to herself, grabbing some oranges, bananas, and lettuces. 'Ooh, look at the time!' A large clock at the distant checkout showed she had taken nearly half a minute already.

'Sweets. I must get the boys some sweeties!' Tina said. The trouble was, sweets were three aisles away. The aisles were narrow. So she had to barge her way through.

'Excuse me. Excuse me. So sorry. Everso sorry. Excuse me. Oh dear,' she said. Supermarket trolleys aren't designed for the tight wheelies Tina was making. She was burning black rubber marks on the white floor. She ran over the toes of a six-year-old customer, who screamed, not having learned any self-control yet. I blame his parents.

She pinned a pensioner up against the special offer tuna. Many tins toppled upon his bald old head. She caught the corner of a freezer cabinet, bounced off that, found herself in a straight section and belted down twenty yards to where the sweets shone under the lights. She grabbed a dozen boxes of chocolates. She was squeaking with anxiety, like a mouse not knowing which cheese to eat first.

'Oh deary me. What sort does my Tone like best? I think it's these hazelnut ones. Too expensive. Oh, I shouldn't, should I? Oh deary me.' Everything in poor old Tina's life had taught her not to be greedy. She just didn't know *how* to be greedy. Not like me or Anthony. We eat like horses.

'Ooh, help! More than a minute's gone.' She was gasping. What to do next? Head turning from side to side like it was about to fall off, she hurried past the meat section, throwing in five chickens, then on to the ice-cream freezer and rummaged through. Then she stopped, undecided. By now the mother of the squashed six year old was on her heels, followed by the pensioner, clutching his head.

The pensioner was very active. Surprisingly energetic, some of these old codgers. He blocked Tina's path, clutching his bruised head. She recognized him as someone she had seen before.

'It's Tina Bloor, isn't it?' he said.

'That's right. Lovely day, isn't it? But they do say rain's forecast for later,' Tina started saying, out of habit. Then she glanced at the clock ticking away and screamed very loud, with her hands over her ears.

'What the blazes do you think you're doing, woman?' he said.

'Can't stop. Ever so sorry. Can't stop. Oh dear,' Tina said. She began to wail. 'I've got to get on, see, lover. Oh, dear, I wish my Tone and my Tarik were here.' She knew the alcohol section was at the very end of the run, near the check-out. She was a sort of whirling blur. She only knocked over one more person, butting him in the stomach, which is something I had never seen before in my young life, and which proved you don't have to be very big to be lethal.

But waiting at the alcohol section was the store manager, who'd been warned there was a lunatic loose. He grabbed her, and called the police.

We heard them coming, sirens wailing, when we walked away, laughing like drains. I know it was cruel to Tina. But she shouldn't do as she's told so much. Sometimes you have to be cruel to be kind. That's an old grown-up proverb. It would teach her a lesson.

Then we went back to the Home.

'Watch out. The Big Three are coming,' we shouted at the little kids, punching the air and giving them nasty looks. I stabbed the air with a large invisible bayonet, (after chucking some invisible hand-grenades), Anthony mowed people down with an invisible machine-gun, and Maddie practised her strangling-the-invisible-cat routine.

We had a bet going, to see who'd be the first to make one of the little ones wet themselves with fear. The littlies just jeered at us, and we were dying to tell them about what we'd been up to, but we couldn't, because we'd signed a secrecy pact, with a pin, in our own blood.

Nine

I'd still heard nothing from the Dog Whipper. After a couple more weeks I had another meeting with my Link Worker and she said she could now trust me to go to the town alone. I'd tricked her, like I could trick lots of people.

The first place I visited was the cathedral. I hadn't been there for a long time. It was now the middle of November, cold and wet. All the lights were on inside, as I sat down in my usual place, near the font. I liked to sit near the font because that was where babies were baptized. I'd never seen a baptism, and I wasn't baptized myself. I imagined the baby to be all calm, smiling. Maybe they warmed the water, and tested it to be just right with an elbow, the way I saw someone on telly doing it before bathing a baby. I imagined Tarik being baptized as a little brown, smiling baby, kicking his chubby legs. Perfect. It wasn't right that he didn't have a father. As for Tina, she was too soft and stupid. She couldn't stimulate Tarik enough, get his brain going, teach him new things. That's what *I* thought, anyway.

On my roundabout way to the font, I did my usual routine of touching special statues in a certain order, my good-luck routine. Not that it had brought me much luck yet. Then I'd nodded at the Lady with the Sash, who smiled at me and said hello and seemed to want to talk, but I walked past her.

I wouldn't be seen dead talking to someone with a blue rinse, glasses with black rims which made her eyes look like an eagle's, and a tartan kilt. Very uncool.

I thought the Dog Whipper would come to see me. I waited patiently. I only had an hour, and I so needed to talk to him. I wanted to know if he had consulted anyone about how I was going to meet my mum, like he promised. But he didn't appear.

Instead, just as I was about to give up, the Tumbler Monk came looking for me. I'd seen him before, at a distance, but never spoken to him. He came walking up the aisle—on his hands. Then he did a couple of cartwheels, and a handspring, and was standing in front of me, slightly out of breath, but smiling. Quite frankly, I thought he was a bit fat to be doing all the acrobatics—fat like me.

He had a very big head and a pudding-basin haircut, so that his light brown hair was chopped off in a semi-circle above his forehead, making his face like a full moon. He was wearing a brown monk's cassock.

'My lady!' he said, and took a bow. I'd never been called a lady before. 'I have come to see you in the place of my good friend, Mr Dog Whipper. He is away. He said to me that you might be visiting us. Welcome to our magnificent cathedral, my lady.'

I noticed that he had a strong French accent. Then I remembered that the legend about him was French—that he had come to the cathedral from France but couldn't follow the Latin they used in those days to worship in, so he had never been to any of the services.

The other monks thought it was a bit funny, him not joining in, and one of them spied on him and saw him worshipping the Virgin Mary by doing juggling and tumbling tricks in front of her altar, instead of praying. So then the masons carved him on the north side of the nave, showing him balancing on his chin, upside down above the head of someone playing the violin. It was like a circus trick—one man balancing on the head of another.

The masons carved a Virgin Mary on the opposite side of the nave, for him to look at, but it's gone now.

'Where's the Dog Whipper? I haven't seen him for weeks. When's he coming back?'

'I do not know, my lady. I too have not seen him—for two or three weeks. Sometimes he goes away. It is when he is making—how do you say it in English?—a very important business. But I am here to entertain you . . . ' and he did a backwards somersault, and then the splits.

He was about thirty years old, but acted like a kid. I was surprised how supple he was, considering the blubber on him. I could just about still do the splits, but I was only twelve. Nearly thirteen, now.

'Is there any way I can get a message to the Dog Whipper? He's ignoring me, for some reason,' I said.

'I do not know, my lady. I will call the senior Green Man. Sometimes, Mr Dog Whipper leaves with him an address—what do you call it, an address to send messages on to?'

'A forwarding address?'

'C'est ça. A forwarding address.'

He put two fingers to his mouth and gave a loud whistle. I say it was loud, because it nearly deafened me. But no one else seemed to notice. Certainly not the Lady with the Sash, who sat reading quietly in a corner.

Next thing I knew, there was a rustling sound, like leaves, and one of the cathedral's Green Men—the one from near the Lady Chapel—came lumbering towards us.

He moved very slowly and painfully and when he got closer, I could see why. He had to drag his roots with him.

He had bright green leaves growing out of his head instead of hair, his body was a tree trunk, and from his big mouth came four thick branches, springing out and growing even as I watched. At first, I had retreated, because I thought they were snakes.

I told you before I'm not scared of anything, but that was one of my fibs. I'm scared of snakes, even when they are behind glass.

The Green Man finally came to a halt in front of us. He was huge.

'This young lady has come looking for our friend the Dog Whipper. Has he left any messages with you, or an address where she might write to him?' said the Tumbler.

When the Green Man spoke, his voice was like wind in the trees. Very soothing. 'No, no one has seen him. But he will return. He always returns,' he said.

I looked doubtful.

'Keep one of my leaves. It will stay green until the Dog Whipper returns,' he said. 'When he is about to come back, it will fade and die.' A single bright-green leaf, nearly round in shape, with a little brown stalk, fluttered down from one of his branch-tips, and I picked it up off the floor, and put it in the back pocket of my jeans.

I like trees, and I started to like the Green Man, now I wasn't so scared of him. The guide book had said he was a very ancient fertility symbol, and that he dated from before the Christians came to England.

'How old are you?' I asked him.

'That depends,' he said.

'On what?'

'Well, the carvings of me and the others—there are more than forty of us Green Men here—are only about seven or eight hundred years old, I forget, they were made so recently . . .'

'Only,' I said.

'But before that, long before that, we were in other religions and beliefs and we are what you call timeless, I suppose.'

'Eternal,' said the Tumbler, as if he liked the idea.

'Can I climb you?' I asked. I liked climbing trees.

'Better than that. I will lift you,' he said, and before I knew it he had bent down from the middle of his trunk and lowered a strong branch and two smaller branches lifted me on to it and then he stood up and I was twenty feet in the air, so that I had a wonderful view of the ceiling and the fourteen angels on the wall opposite. I felt perfectly safe. What was even better, I didn't feel heavy, because the Green Man was so strong. There was no one in this secluded part of the cathedral, so no one saw me flying through the air.

Just then the angels, who had been quiet every other time I had been in the cathedral, started to play. It was a dance, with drum beats, trumpets, bagpipes, sounds like violins and flutes. There was singing too. Young choirboys singing. The Green Man danced with me and I was high up in the cathedral, being whirled around, feeling very special and lucky, just for a moment. For about the first time ever, actually.

Then, from down below us, I heard a bad-tempered voice, grumbling.

'That Godwin, he's never happy,' said the Green Man.

It was Matthew Godwin, whose tomb was in the north wall. I don't think he liked the music. In fact, I knew he didn't.

'Do you not appreciate that I am the Master of Music here, and that there must be no performance without me?' he said, in a cold voice. I looked down. I could see him now. He had a white ruff around his neck, and tight trousers. Over them he wore a bright red gown. He looked very young to be a Master of Music. 'Young, pious, and gentle; a genius, bachelor of music, very worthy and very learned,' the inscription on his tomb said. It didn't say how bad-tempered he was.

'No one listens to you any more. When you died, your powers ceased with you,' said the Green Man, hopping from one leg to another. The angels continued playing. 'We, on the other hand, are timeless.'

'Eternal,' said the Tumbler, who was doing hand-springs in time to the music, and then juggling with five little leather balls he had produced from his pocket.

Matthew Godwin had been Master of the Music both here and at Canterbury Cathedral. I knew that. He was a Tudor. I expect he must have met Queen Elizabeth. The first one, I mean. He died very young.

I was quite interested in the idea of all the cathedral's inhabitants arguing amongst themselves, like we do at the Home. I began to wonder who was top-dog among them. At the Home, it is Maddie, because she is oldest.

I wondered if the Dog Whipper was top dog.

But then it was time for a service, and the angels stopped playing. The Tumbler went back to his upside-down position on his corbel, the Green Man put me down quickly and disappeared, and Matthew Godwin climbed back into his tomb, still complaining.

I walked over to it. I worked out from the dates there that he had died when he was only seventeen years and five months old. Not very much older than me. I wondered how you got to be a Master of Music when you are only seventeen. He must have been some kind of genius.

'I was, a true genius,' he whispered from inside his grave, as if he could read my mind, which made me jump. 'No one appreciated me then, or ever since, alas.'

I had to go back to the Home after that. As I caught the bus, I felt in my jeans back pocket for the leaf given to me by the Green Man. It was still bright green and that made me sad, because it meant the Dog Whipper was not coming back soon.

Ten

'I want to play another trick on somebody. Like Tina's supermarket dash. Bella, what shall we do? You're the one with all the wicked ideas.'

It was Anthony, one Sunday morning. He was bored, and had been awake for a long while. But I still wanted to sleep.

'Go away. It's too early,' I said. No one else was up— not even the two duty staff, who sleep one each end of the corridor.

Anthony stood in my doorway. He was all blubber, blond bristle haircut, and yellow eyelashes. He had hold of his revolting mud-coloured fluffy bird by its beak. He had on his blue pyjamas. The trousers were coming unhitched and his fat tummy was showing. I looked away. The last thing I wanted to see was Anthony with his kit off.

'Think of something,' he said, and shuffled back to his room, holding up his pyjamas.

So I lay there, and thought of something.

I decided we'd all go to town on the next Saturday, which is market day. The pubs are open all afternoon and the drunks spill out onto the pavements. They really do say

'Ooh arr', and 'That's proper job, my beauty', but I expect it's just for the tourists.

I was looking for people begging. I wanted the three most ugly, smelly ones I could find. 'And they've got to be drunk,' I said.

Maddie said that in the begging league, Britain was European champion. We won on the numbers of them, with extra style points for dirt, whiskers, stink, dribble, and bad teeth.

'We want some old ones. These are much too young,' I said, when she pointed out two, with their dogs on strings, quite near the cathedral. They looked only in their twenties, and quite healthy.

We found a promising old man lying in a doorway in the main street, fast asleep. Anthony bent over him, sniffed and said, 'Sorry, not smelly enough. Too clean.'

Maddie came across a crusty bag-lady but when Anthony cross-questioned her she said no, she did not drink, that drink was ruination indeed, oh Lord, and was he interested in becoming a Christian like her? She tried to hold his hand for prayers, being down on her knees already.

'Not alcoholic enough, that one. Sorry,' Anthony said. He pulled himself free and walked away, after giving her his nastiest smile, which I'd been teaching him. With his blond crew-cut and fat legs, it made him look like a concentration-camp commander. Junior version of.

At last, down near the railway station, we found three filthy, old, and very drunk men sharing a huge cardboard box. They were sleepy, and quite good-natured.

'They'll do,' Anthony said.

Next thing we knew, the three men were staggering towards us. Their names were Ted, Ron, and Frank.

Ted was a tubby, red Father Christmas, Ron was thin

and part bald, part shaggy. Where hair grew it was in tufts, mostly from his ears.

Frank's eyes rolled round, loose in their sockets, which was a bit scary, but otherwise he seemed more or less in control of himself, considering how drunk he was. He had a way of clearing his throat which made you feel a bit sick, and then he'd gob a lump of yellow phlegm at the pavement, saying cheerfully, 'Better out than in', except that sometimes he'd miss and spatter his trousers, or anyone who happened to be nearby.

They were swigging Special Brew, from cans. We all went into the railway station, and boarded a train without tickets, which was easy. We told Ted, Ron, and Frank that we were taking them to a big tramps' party, one specially arranged for them by our Youth Club (which didn't exist). They believed us and liked the idea.

'Nice kids, you are. Haven't been to a party for donkey's years,' said Frank, falling in a heap into a seat in one of the First Class carriages. The other two sat down beside him and began to smoke the Old Shag black tobacco we'd brought for them. (We'd nicked it from the gardener at the Home.)

Soon you couldn't read the No Smoking sign in the First Class carriage for the smoke the tramps were putting out. Ted belched, all cheerful, and looked around him for a conversation but the other passengers refused to look at him except for a small boy in a blazer and grey flannel trousers, who was quickly told not to.

Frank's eyes went wibble-wobble in their oversized sockets. At one point, the right one was rolling clockwise and the left anti-clockwise. It only took five minutes for the other passengers to leave the carriage, and the train had barely pulled out of the station.

'Where've they all gone? There's no decent talk in these First Class compartments,' Ron complained when he woke from a snooze which had stretched him over the seat. The last he remembered, he'd been leaning against a man in a posh double-breasted suit.

'First Class people are so polite. They'd rather do anything than have a row,' Maddie said. 'But they aren't so slow in complaining.' She'd spotted a ticket collector coming down the corridor.

We quickly made up a story that we had to go up to the restaurant car.

'Bye now. Be good boys and girls,' said Ron, smiling and lighting up another fag.

'We'll try not to be,' we said. We scarpered and hid in the lavatories, got out at the next station, boarded another train and got back to town, so we never knew what happened to the tramps, which was disappointing, because I'd planned to take them to all sorts of smart places and see what happened. Like posh restaurants and hotels and places like that.

If only we'd had lots of money, we could have paid for them and seen how the rich people liked sharing their fancy restaurants. It would have been a laugh.

'That trick was only just getting going,' said Anthony. 'Think of some other ones, Bella,' so I did.

We got hold of a catalogue from a sex shop and a credit card we borrowed from the Home's office and ordered a black see-through nylon nightie and one or two other things which I'd better not mention for one of the care staff—the woman with the biggest moustache. Unfortunately we were unable to see her open the parcel.

We bought a local paper and looked in the 'Lonely Hearts' column—Men Looking For Women. Then Maddie and I rang a couple of them, one each, and pretended to be nineteen years old. The two men—both were in their thirties—sounded interested, so we arranged to meet them, separately.

Then we went to the restaurant and looked through the window and laughed at them, waiting at their separate tables. Maddie and I had a bet on which one would hang on the longest, waiting.

Mine had curly yellow hair, obviously dyed, and smoked non-stop. He drank a whole bottle of red wine while he waited. He had big, fat, wide lips. Maddie's man wore trainers, and a sort of tracksuit. He looked quite fit, and would have been fanciable, except for his skin, which was like an erupted volcano.

'Mine's Donald Duck, yours is Mount Etna,' I said. Maddie laughed. Donald left first, looking fed up, so I lost the bet. Etna hung on for a while, looking at his watch, a disappointed man. If they'd talked to each other, instead of staring into their drinks, they might have discovered they'd been conned. Anyway, they were only after one thing, I expect.

For her next trick, by putting on a grown-up voice, Maddie ordered a taxi to take the three little kids in the Home to a special Christmas surprise treat—all they could eat at McDonald's and a chance to meet their favourite boy band—and then we watched them burst into tears when the taxi was sent away again by the staff, just when the driver had got their hopes up.

'That'll teach them to be so cheeky,' said Anthony but I suddenly felt a bit sorry for them, although I didn't say so. I decided it wasn't fair to play tricks on children, from now on. Only on grown-ups.

We did a few things around the Home, but only ones that we knew we couldn't be caught for. Old tricks out of the text-book, like putting the bucket of water balanced on the top edge of a half-open door, so that it falls on the person coming in.

It was the head of the Home, a woman who usually has quite a good sense of humour, but who this time didn't see the joke at all, standing there dripping with her clothes soaked. She went so red with anger that I thought she'd start steaming. She wanted to know who had done it, of course, and none of us owned up, so all eight residents had to do without puddings for a week.

'That's not fair,' said the little kids.

'Life's not fair,' is what we said, which is only what we had learned from adults.

Then we did a few things at night involving the staff beds—like putting slugs in them, doing the sheets so that your feet couldn't reach to the end of the bed, and then we found out how to turn off all the electricity so that everyone blundered about in the dark for a few minutes, and one of the staff tripped over a chair and banged her shin, which made her come out with all sorts of swear words we never thought she knew.

But we were getting too many punishments at the Home and then they threatened us with not getting any Christmas presents.

Anyway, I was beginning to get tired of tricks on other people. I was getting so I had to be really bad. The time had come when I had to take Tarik, and have him for myself.

I wanted him for my Christmas present. Nobody wanted *me*, I knew that. If someone had wanted me, I wouldn't have been in the Children's Home, would I? I couldn't resist it any more.

If only the Dog Whipper hadn't gone away, I probably wouldn't have done it. He'd deserted me, like everybody else, and I couldn't be good any more.

Eleven

Before I could take Tarik, I had to study how mothers looked after their children. I had to find when the right moment would be . . . the moment when they took their eyes off them. I had to get in Tina's good books, too.

Have you ever stood and watched mothers with little children? It's very interesting. I think women should pass an exam before they're allowed to become mothers. You have to take a test to drive a car. There should be a mothering test, too. My mum wouldn't have passed. She'd have crashed the car before even leaving the test station. She'd probably have run over the driving instructor as well.

My dad once told me something about my mother. It was soon after they got divorced, and he wanted me on his side. He said that when he first met her, before she had me, she was very vain. She used to get all dressed up in her best clothes and parade up and down the High Street of the town where they lived, with her little dog, a toy poodle. The poodle wore a pink ribbon in its white fur, just like my mum did in her dyed blonde hair—she was a blonde in those days.

Apparently, she was so busy parading up and down and making eyes at the young men watching that she didn't see a newspaper delivery van run over her little poodle—it was called Jackie—and squash it to death. She carried on walking, tugging at the lead, dragging the dead dog behind her.

'She dragged it all the way down the High Street and it was only when she turned round to parade back again that she noticed Jackie was a gonner,' my dad said, laughing nastily.

Well, can you imagine having that vain and absent-minded a person for your mother? She should never have been allowed to have children.

The written babycare test first, then the practical bit.

What do babies need most? a) Cuddles? b) A nice bottle of warm milk? c) Plonking in front of the telly?

Your two year old keeps coughing at night. Do you: a) Roll over and go back to sleep? b) Call an ambulance? c) Give him a spoonful of cough medicine and bring him into bed with you, to comfort him?

Say in 500 words why you wanted a baby in the first place. Be truthful. You get extra marks if you can prove that you thought about it and asked the right questions beforehand.

Why does it take babies so long to grow into adults? How have you got ready for the job of bringing them up? Can you last the full course?

The practical test would need a real baby, a borrowed one, say six months old. You'd have tests in: feeding it, changing a full nappy, rocking to sleep, holding, listening for the baby crying.

There'd be a sound chamber and you would have to listen to a baby screaming (only a tape, repeating, so as not to make it cruel on the baby) and you'd have to put up with it for ten minutes without shouting at the baby, saying you were going to hit it, or putting your hands over your ears.

You'd have to be woken twenty times in one night, and they'd measure your heartbeat and all your stress levels to see if you could stand it.

There'd be a smackometer and every time you smacked your child you'd get a written warning. Three times in one week and you would have to go to special mothering classes, compulsory.

When I was in town, I studied the young mothers. I learned how you can smoke with one hand, feed the baby with the other, keep yacking to your friend—all at the same time. And listen to Radio One, too.

I learned the language of don't and stop. Don't do this, don't do that, stop this, stop that. I learned about how to count to three, like 'I'm warning you. Stop doing that before I count to three, or you'll get a smack. One, two, three . . . '

I learned how to send a young child crazy. You ask it crazy questions like 'Do you want a smack?' ('Yes, please, Mummy, I'd love one, right on my bare botty') and 'Do you love Mummy?' Well, there's only one answer to that, isn't there—if you want to survive?

I studied how mums look at their children. Frowning, bored, glaring, angry, a lot of the time. Just once or twice you'd see a mum and a baby looking at each other, close up, the baby in the mother's arms, maybe, relaxed, and the look would be so calm and good, and the mother would be copying the baby's expression, so the mum was the baby's mirror, really. And then I knew that I had never had that mirror and it hurt so much I had to run away before I started howling.

Each day I would look at the leaf in my back pocket and each day it would be bright green. Then one day, as I was sitting in the Cathedral Close, watching the mums doing their Christmas shopping with their little children, and seeing how the kids wanted things all the time and how this made the mums so cross because they couldn't give them what they wanted, I reached for the leaf and it had turned brown.

The Dog Whipper was coming back!

I was so excited. I looked around me. It was a drizzly afternoon and the light was fading. Soon I'd have to go back to the Home. Where was he?

An old man came to sit near me on the bench. He was dressed in those horrible clothes old men wear—sort of light brown nylon trousers with a straight crease, tight in the arse, sensible black shiny laceless shoes with non-slip soles, one of those turquoise green weatherproof walking jackets, with the hood up, so I couldn't see his face. I paid no attention.

Then he said something. 'I see you are watching the young mothers, Bella,' and it was the Dog Whipper's voice. His calm, kind voice.

'I never knew you could disguise yourself,' I said, edging across the seat so that I could be close to him.

'Sometimes it can be useful,' he said.

'Where have you been? It's been weeks since I saw you. I went to the cathedral but you weren't there. I met the Tumbler, the Green Man, Matthew Godwin. I heard the angels play.'

'I have been away. I have been on a mission. I am afraid it has been taking me longer than I thought. I came back today to see you. What are you planning, Bella? I have a feeling it is not a good thing.'

I wasn't going to tell him about my plan to steal Tarik. I used to trust the Dog Whipper and tell him everything, but since he went away and left me I thought he was just like everybody else, all those grown-ups who promise something but then let you down.

'You might at least have come to me in a dream, like before,' I said.

'Ah! The importance of dreams!' was all he said. Then he asked me again, all serious, why I was studying the young mothers.

'I want to learn why they are doing all the wrong things, some of them,' I said. 'When I have children, I want to do it right.'

'I'm sure you will do your best. Most people do their best, you know.'

'Well, sometimes their best isn't good enough,' I said. He didn't say anything to that, but turned his head and pulled back his hood a bit and looked at me, hard.

'Anyway, I don't suppose I'll ever be a mother. To be a mother, you have to find a boyfriend, or a husband, and no one would want me, because of my blubber,' I said.

'What is blubber?' he said.

'Fat. Don't you know that? The fat bits—my arms, and legs, and bum and my fat face. It's so ugly, being fat.'

'I don't think you are ugly,' he said, but I just snorted.

'What do you know about anything? You're hundreds of years out of fashion, you are.'

'Blubber, blubber, blubber,' he said softly to himself, as if remembering this new word. Then he asked if it had another meaning.

'No. Just fat,' I said. Then I remembered, in some book I had read, the girl in it blubbed when her pet rabbit died. 'It can mean crying, too. To blub is to cry,' I said.

'So, a blubber is a person who cries,' he said.

'Yes. Or you might call her a blubber*er*,' I said.

'I see.' He was thinking, I could tell.

'I never blub,' I said. 'Not any more, I don't. Not for years, now.'

He tried to catch my eye, but I looked down at the wet grass, and chewed my bubblegum even harder.

We sat there for a minute or two, in the drizzle, with the street lights coming on all around the Cathedral Close, and I wanted so much to be friends like we once were, but something had changed. It was like he was far away, even though he sat next to me.

Then it was time for me to catch the bus back to the Home.

'Will you come to see me again?' I begged.

'I cannot say. That depends upon you,' he said, all serious still.

That wasn't good enough. It all depended on me!

'I thought I had a friend,' I said, standing up. 'I suppose you're just another one who let me down.'

'I am a friend,' he said and then we went our separate ways. I stalked back to the Home, angry with him. He walked slowly back down the path to the cathedral and his little rooms above the nave.

Back at the Home, I got into Tina's good books by being nice to her when she came to tidy my room, and then I started asking after Tarik and badgering her to let me come and play with him.

She let me come, straight after school, the next day. All I had to do was wait until her back was turned. It was about ten to four, I remember, just getting dark, and she was starting to make his tea. It was beans on toast with a boiled egg, and a glass of milk. She was in the little kitchen, and the radio was on. More of her horrible Radio Two music.

'I'll get your coat and you can come out with me. We'll go and see the ducks in the village pond,' I said to Tarik, who trusted me. He was pleased.

'Duck ducks,' I said. I found his little blue coat with the yellow collar, and his red wellies.

'Quack quack quack,' I said. I flapped my arms, like they were wings. Tarik laughed.

I told Tina we would be back in five minutes. 'That's fine, my love,' she said. She believed me. I always knew she was stupid.

At last, I had Tarik all to myself. And we weren't going to see any ducks.

Twelve

At first, Tarik thought it was all an exciting game. I led him down the lane to where I knew there would be a bus very soon. He liked buses and I let him sit near the front, where he could see out.

We went into the town, then changed buses and went towards the sea.

'Seaside,' said Tarik. It was dark by now but I expect he thought we'd be going paddling, or something.

I'd been saving up my pocket money, and had stashed away enough food and drink to last us for two or three days, if we were careful. Tarik was still in nappies at night and I'd nicked some from Tina's house. I had planned everything. Or so I thought.

When the bus reached the seaside town we got out but instead of going down to the sea we walked up a little country road for about a mile. It was properly dark by now but I'd brought a torch and Tarik thought it was all a big adventure, especially when I told him we were looking for treasure.

We came to the old quarry where they got the stone for the cathedral, hundreds of years ago. It's all in the cathedral guidebook—how they hauled the limestone by cart through the lanes and by boat round the coast and up the estuary. Tons and tons of stone from deep underground.

Nowadays the quarry is worked out and it's just a tourist attraction, with big iron bars to keep people out at night. But I knew how to get in.

I lifted Tarik up where there was a space between the bars and the cave roof, just big enough to squeeze through. He was as agile as a monkey and climbed down the other side. I passed him my bag and the sleeping bag and candles and everything I had brought. The caves are shut to tourists over the winter and I thought we'd be safe here for days.

Then I had to climb in. I thought I wouldn't make it. I had to take a deep breath in and push through, scraping my shoulders and fat tummy so that I was bleeding when I finally got through, with Tarik waiting patiently for me. He didn't seem at all scared in the dark.

'Look. Birdies!' he said, pointing at something flying past without making any noise. It wasn't a bird, it was a bat. I shone the torch at it, hoping to frighten it away, but it kept flitting in and out of the beam, quite close. I had to turn the torch off, to stop it, and for a while we were in complete darkness.

It was really cold down there. I hadn't realized how wet it would be. There was a steady drip, drip of water and Tarik began to grizzle when he tripped over and fell into a puddle as we made our way deep under the hillside. I had to get out the first bar of chocolate I'd brought with me, to quieten him down. Bribery. Stop crying and you'll get some, I said. Adults use bribery like that. Tarik knew the score, and stopped.

I shone the torch all round. There were pillars of limestone left to support the ceiling, and the quarriers had cut their names on some, hundreds of years ago, in spindly writing, all angles. I thought of them underground, with only candles, no electricity, as they cut and picked at the rock.

I wanted to find a dry place, where we could settle, but there wasn't anywhere. All you could hear was the water dripping, and sometimes the flutter of bats' wings. Then Tarik started. It was what I was dreading.

'I want to go home now,' he said. 'I want my mummy.'

I hated that word, 'Mummy'. It spelt trouble for me.

I wrapped him up warm in the sleeping bag and sang to him. I sang every song I knew, pop songs mostly. I realized that I didn't remember any nursery rhymes which Tarik would know. I asked him what he liked singing.

'Black sheep. Little star,' he said, shivering a bit.

'That shouldn't be difficult. They're both the same tune,' I said.

I sat down on a square piece of stone and cradled him, swinging backwards and forwards gently as I sang the silly words. Imagine asking a sheep if it had any wool. Imagine singing to a twinkling star.

'Again,' he said, each time I stopped. I began to realize the biggest problem with looking after little children—boredom. It was like he couldn't get enough of the songs, but repeating the words was driving me mad.

It must have been half an hour before he finally went to sleep, in my arms, and when I tried to lay him down he woke up, grizzled, and complained about the cold. I had to start all over again.

I've done it. I've got him all to myself, I thought. Then I thought, *Now what?* and almost panicked. The truth is, I hadn't thought what to do next, after taking Tarik. I'd somehow convinced myself that everything would be OK, like in a fairy story. But life isn't like a fairy story. Fairy stories are only for children, and for mad people, who believe them. Maybe I was mad. I didn't feel mad—because for once I had done something I'd wanted to, planned it all and carried it through. I'd, like, taken charge

77

of myself. But I hadn't thought of the consequences. To hell with it. I had to just enjoy what I had, now. Or try to.

I didn't have a watch. I was beginning to be tired—and cold. It came from sitting still in the same position on the wet stone. I was beginning to feel sorry for myself, and lonely. I hadn't told Maddie or Anthony what I was planning to do. I thought that the police would be asking them lots of questions by now.

I didn't let myself think about what Tina would be going through. I put my cheek against Tarik's and felt his warm breath, very regular. I liked to think I was protecting him. His eyes, with their lovely dark lashes, were closed. His lids were a little bit shiny, very smooth—almost like they had been oiled. I touched one, and he blinked.

Then I put Tarik down and lay beside him and shut my eyes and fell asleep.

The nightmares began quite quickly. There was a gang of quarriers, all men, standing around me, silently. They had their picks and saws for cutting the limestone in their hands. There were about twenty of them, in a big circle. I could only see their legs, bodies, and arms. It was as if the light from my candle faded when it got to their heads. I knew they must have heads, but not being able to see their expressions was what was frightening. That, and the fact that they wouldn't speak. Not even the boy ones, the ones my own age.

'I'm not staying here long. Sorry if I came without an invitation,' I said.

Silence.

'Are you ghosts, or real?' I asked, because I couldn't tell any more if I was dreaming.

Silence. Their bodies swayed from side to side, like reeds in a wind, but made no sound.

I switched on the torch and shone it at the biggest one. I saw his face, with its old-fashioned beard round the edge of his big jaw. I think you call it a chin-strap beard. I saw his thin mouth, shut tight as a trap. But he had no eyes. Where his eyes should have been were just two dark holes, very deep. Like looking down a well. I thought I was tumbling into the holes, falling for ever. I screamed.

That woke Tarik up, and he started crying. I shone the torch around, but the miners had gone. It took me an hour to get Tarik to sleep again. Then, just as I fell asleep too, the miners came back. In the same big circle, just watching me. Except they had no eyes to watch with.

After that, I didn't dare sleep again. To tell the truth, I didn't really know what was real and what was dreams, any more. Maybe I was mad, after all. Like my mother.

In the cathedral, I had watched people praying. They are very discreet about it, muttering to the god they believe in, asking for things, hoping for things.

It was time for me to pray, but I didn't know how. Nobody had taught me. What did I really want? Sleep, that was it. And an answer to the big problem of what to do next. I hadn't thought what to do after I took Tarik. I hadn't figured out how I would get away with it.

The only person I could think of praying to was the Dog Whipper. I put my hands together, like I'd seen the people do in the cathedral.

'Dear Dog Whipper,' I began in a low voice, so as not to wake Tarik, 'I know that you think what I've done is wrong. Please forgive me and help me to sleep. Tell the quarrier ghosts to go away. Give me advice on what to do with Tarik, so that I can look after him for ever and he will love me and not want his mummy any more. With all my love, Bella.'

Then I curled up and fell asleep, but only for a few minutes because I woke up scared and there were the quarrier ghosts, silent as ever, eyeless as ever, standing around me, swaying. There was no message from the Dog Whipper.

'Speak! Say something!' I shouted but they stood there with their picks and saws and their beards and old-fashioned clothes. Then Tarik woke up, of course, and he had wet himself and I had to change his nappy and I never did get any more sleep that night.

'Go away, Dog Whipper, and don't ever come back. I don't believe in you any more,' I said.

'Where's doggies?' said Tarik.

'Nowhere. No one. No doggies,' I said.

Thirteen

In the morning it was colder still. There'd been a frost outside. It was only a few weeks until Christmas, and it looked like snow was on the way.

I unwrapped our breakfast—chocolate, bread and butter, an orange each—and Tarik ate all his. For the time being, he seemed to have forgotten about his mummy.

'Where's treasure?' he asked.

We were in a gallery quite near the entrance, and a little light let us see the grey walls and the pools of water. To keep him amused, I said we had to dig for the treasure. I'd brought an old trowel with me, and Tarik was quite happy for a while, picking up bits of stone and looking underneath. I turned it into a sweetie hunt, and hid bits of chocolate. Each time he found one, he laughed and ate it. But I knew this game couldn't last for long. We were running out of chocolate.

I tried to think of other games he could play. He was too little for 'I Spy' or word games. I knew how to look after him—like, changing his nappy, feeding him, keeping him warm—but I couldn't think of ways to play with him, and he was getting bored. To tell you the truth, so was I.

Then came the danger word again, 'Mummy'. Something had made him think of her, and he started to grizzle.

'We'll go and see Mummy later,' I said, which was a lie, but it made him stop crying for a bit.

It was now mid-morning. I turned on my Walkman radio to find out the time, and tuned in to the local radio station. Then I heard the news. They'd made Tarik the number one item. They used words like 'abduction' and 'manhunt' and 'fears are growing' and then there was a policewoman appealing to a 'twelve-year-old girl' to bring Tarik back. They didn't name me.

Then there was a brief interview with Tina. 'Please, please bring my little boy back. He needs me, he needs his brother Tony. We're all he's got. Please bring him back safely. Don': be afraid that I'll be angry. Just bring him back. Please,' and then she started sobbing.

I wasn't sorry for her. Not at all. She should have taken better care of him. I didn't let Tarik know he was in the news. But they'd given a description of him and me and I knew we might be recognized.

My plan was to wait until dark and then leave the quarries, especially as I couldn't stand another cold night there, with the staring ghosts. I thought we might find a farmyard to sleep in, some nice warm hay instead of the cold, wet, cave floors. But it was only mid-morning.

I told Tarik stories, with little furry bunnies in, and cats and mice and all those sort of things which children like. All with happy endings. We sat wrapped in blankets, both inside the sleeping bag, and it wasn't too bad but I began to realize that I wasn't going to make it through to the evening.

The truth was that I just didn't know what to do with Tarik. I just didn't have enough inside me for him— enough games, stories, talk, maybe love, even. I couldn't be his mummy. I thought I would have enough for him, but I didn't. I was running on empty.

So when he began to call for her again, around lunchtime, I got angry and told him to shut up, which only made him worse. He began to howl properly, which made me just want to run away and leave him, to get away from the noise.

I nearly smacked him. I didn't, but it was close. I'd watched those young mothers sitting around the Cathedral Close, nagging and smacking their kids, and I thought I was going to do the same. I felt so ashamed, because I couldn't manage Tarik. I'd really wanted to be a better mother than all the ones I'd studied, and I couldn't do it. I felt bad, really bad, about that.

I sat there, listening to him howling, and knew I had to give him back. It was like saying hello to the old Bella, again. The Bella who never got what she wanted, or needed.

I told him we were going back to his mum, which shut him up at once and I wiped his tears away with a tissue and we climbed out of the quarry the way we had come in— through the gap at the top of the bars—and walked down the lane until we came to a telephone box in the village.

I dialled 999 and asked for the police and they came to get me and Tarik pretty quick, with two police cars. The old ladies behind their net curtains in the village must have had a thrill when the cars pulled up, tyres screeching. They separated me and Tarik, one to each car, and that was the last I saw of him. I kept my head down, so as not to watch them taking him away.

I cried then, when his police car went one way—back to his mummy—and mine went to the police station. It was the first time I'd cried for ages. Years. I thought I'd forgotten how to do it, to be honest. The nice policewoman with me in the back of the car held my hand, and that made me cry more, so that I couldn't stop.

* * *

They put me in the Secure Unit, after that.

No one likes being locked up. Certainly not mixed-up twelve-year-old girls. The trouble was, there was nowhere else that the courts could be sure would stop me from doing something wicked again.

My Link Worker came to see me at the Unit, in the first week. She was full of soft words and regrets and said I'd let her down and stuff like that, so I refused to speak to her, in the barred interview room, with the screws listening in.

She was a hand-wringer and sigher, my Link Worker. She had her hanky out and kept dabbing her eyes, almost like a sign for me to cry, but I wasn't going to. Not in front of her.

'This is the last port of call, Bella,' she said, as if we were on some cruise. 'We've tried foster care. The ''difficult foster'' scheme, with relief care as an option. You're getting too old for adoption, with your record. It would be very hard to find someone who'd have you, I'm afraid. Your mother certainly can't have you. Your father's out of the question. You've no other close relatives. The Children's Home can't have you back, now that you took Tarik. They'd fear you'd abscond, anyway. You have to be somewhere where they can contain you, and you can have treatment. You need help, Bella.'

I suppose she meant counselling or child psychiatry and all those other therapies that I'd had a go at along the line—play therapy, art therapy, drama therapy, family therapy, this therapy, that therapy. When I was little I had sand therapy, in a sand tray. I flooded it, then threw wet sand at the therapist. I thought all therapy was a complete waste of time, if you want to know. Well, it might be OK for others, but not for me. One therapist called me 'hostile', just because I spat at him when he used big words.

The only thing I'd allow myself to ask my Link Worker was 'How's Tarik?' and she said he seemed to be OK, and that he'd had a check-up in hospital, but that Tina was on medication to help her sleep and was off work sick, indefinitely. For the first time, I did feel a bit sorry for her.

When my Link Worker tried asking me too many things I shouted at her in the biggest voice I could make and the screws came running. I told them I wanted to go back to my room. End of interview.

My room wasn't too bad. I liked to spend a lot of time there, even though I was locked in, and even though there was a spy hole in the door, and a closed-circuit camera in one corner. The room was painted pink, my favourite colour, and the bed was comfortable, with a snuggly duvet. There was a round window, high up, and through it I could see an oak tree, outside, beyond the shiny security fence. It kept me going, that oak tree. It made me think of the Green Man, and of his big strong branches lifting me up, high into the air.

For the first week, I wasn't allowed any shoelaces or belts—anything I could hang myself with—but that didn't bother me.

I sat there for hours on end, writing my diary. I could watch telly there, and play video games, and read. I didn't want to mix with the other girls in the unit, but I had to.

There was Karin, in for drug-dealing. Mandy, who'd been a child-prostitute and had fallen out with her pimp, and was there for her own protection more than anything. There was a skinny little black girl from Somalia who was an illegal immigrant and had been done for picking pockets. There were two girls from the north. One had stabbed an old lady, the other one had set fire to her boyfriend's house when he dumped her.

There were boys there, too. I didn't fancy any of them and, needless to say, they didn't fancy me, with my blubber. All they wanted to do was eat, play computer games, go down the gym and pump iron and have long games of football every evening under the floodlights.

The screws weren't too bad. You could talk to them easier than you could talk to the other inmates. There was one man who taught me to play chess and then we got talking about writing and he lent me a book on it, not forcing it on me, just an easy sort of casual offer, which I took up.

But I hated the shiny brown wire fences, thirty feet high, and the floodlights and the jangle of keys, keys, keys—keys for everything, which of course none of us inmates were allowed to touch. Each member of staff had a panic button, too, strapped to their belts, in case someone attacked them.

There were some dangerous kids in there, no doubt about it, with lots of violent form, much more than me. Attempted murder. Rape. Some things which they wouldn't talk about. I was scared of them, which was why I spent as much time as I could in my room. I wasn't the hard girl any more, not in their company.

It was pointless trying to think about legging it. You were always watched; there were twice as many staff as kids. No one had ever escaped. It cost more than the most expensive hotel in England to keep each one of us there, the staff said.

We could make phone calls. Not that I had anyone to telephone, although I did ring Maddie and Anthony at the Home, just to say hello, but things were different, now. To start with, someone was listening in to my conversation. Then, Maddie seemed distant, and Anthony couldn't think of what to say. They knew I wasn't coming back, so they couldn't be bothered, I suppose. I'd only rung them because

I couldn't think of anyone else to speak to. I asked them if they had been up to any tricks, like in the days of the Big Three, but they went all vague, as if they didn't know what I was talking about. I think they were a bit scared of me, to tell the truth.

Then, on Christmas Day—imagine it, Christmas Day in the Secure Unit, with a horrible gift from my Link Worker of a blouse, too small so that it made me look even fatter, and it was the wrong colour—I had my first and only telephone call.

'Who is it?' I asked, when they said I should go to the telephone booth.

'A man,' they said, looking me in the eye, questioning me more than answering my questions.

I stood there thinking for a second. My dad? It couldn't be. I hadn't heard from him for years. I went to the booth.

'It's your old friend from the cathedral,' said the Dog Whipper's calm, kind voice down the phone, and that made me burst into tears. I was crying easily, these days.

Fourteen

'I didn't know you could do the telephone,' I said, when I'd stopped sobbing enough. I wasn't used to this sort of crying—from relief, not sadness.

'I can do lots of worldly things,' he said.

'How did you know where I was?'

'Among the things I can do is read. I can read the newspapers.'

'But they never gave my name to the papers.'

'I knew it was you, Bella.'

'So you know what I did, then? I didn't mean any harm to Tarik. I wanted him for myself, is all. I couldn't stop myself.'

'What's done is done, Bella,' he said.

I guessed that one of the screws might be trying to trace the call. They'd want to know why a stranger was ringing me up. They probably thought he was a paedophile and that I'd abducted Tarik for him, or something sick like that. They think the worst things like that, screws do.

'It is Christmas Day and for that reason I wanted to make contact with you . . . best not to visit, I'm afraid,' said the Dog Whipper. I could see that he had a point. They wouldn't have let him in, with his long black cape and long, thick curly grey hair. His little square black skull cap. They'd think he was too weird. Some kind of nutter.

Even when he dressed in disguise, he looked a little odd—his white face, his nearly white hair.

'I'm glad you called,' I said, then started telling him about my new life, and the games of chess I had, and the writing, and how they kept sending me for therapy and how I ran rings round the shrinks. I'd got through two already. 'Possible Personality Disorder,' my notes said, now.

'They're trying to help,' he said, very firmly, but I laughed my loudest laugh, the new, hard-as-nails one I was working on, and swore.

A screw said I had to wind up the telephone call soon. One of the other kids was waiting to ring his mother.

'What would you have liked most, if you could have had anything you liked for Christmas?' the Dog Whipper asked.

'It's like it always is. You know.'

'Tell me.'

'I want my mum,' I said, quietly.

'I don't think I can arrange that, quite,' he said.

'I know you can't. I don't expect miracles,' I said.

'But, Bella, miracles do happen, sometimes,' he said, then he was cut off.

After that I went back to my room. It was mid-morning, on Christmas Day, and I had no one to talk to. I sat in the corner of my room where I thought the closed-circuit camera couldn't see me so well and I cried until lunchtime.

I knew I would have to face the others. It would all be pretend jolly, and there would be turkey and Christmas pudding and games, horrible cheery games. No one should cry in this place. We were all meant to be hard.

I went to the mirror to look at my face and tried to repair the blotches caused by all the crying. I started putting on my new eye-liner. I stared at myself.

Something was different, but I couldn't figure out what it was. Same old fat cheeks, flubbery chin with another flubbery one under it. Same little pink ears and squinty eyes.

But were things the same? Suddenly, I saw it. It was not that I was looking any thinner, but just that I had stopped getting fatter. It was like I had reached my maximum. Either that, or I would have burst.

I realized that I hadn't weighed myself for weeks. I hadn't dared to. Each time I did, the scales showed a few more pounds.

I made my face up, quite excited. Before I went in to lunch I asked to weigh myself. I couldn't believe it. I was four pounds lighter.

As I sat down with the other inmates I tried to figure it out. What had changed? Then I knew. I had been crying a lot. It was like I'd cried away some of my blubber. It was like my tears were made of my fat.

So I cried some more, every day. I was a champion blubberer. It was like a crying diet. I'd just sit there in my room and think about my life and the things which had happened to me and the tears would fall into my pink face towel. If all else failed, I thought of my nan, who had been quite kind to me when I was little, until she died and ended up as dust in an urn on my mum's shelf. Thinking of my nan always worked, and brought the tears back.

I called the towel my crying towel, and I'd put it on the radiator to dry out, afterwards. I licked it. It tasted salty. I slept with it under my pillow. My crying towel. I'd never had a crying towel before.

There were all sorts of tears. Tears of anger, and sadness. I was getting used to those. Tears of relief, very precious ones, when things turned out all right. They should be kept in little glass bottles with the lids screwed down hard, so as not to let the tears evaporate.

The bottle would be kept in a safe place and you could look at the tears and maybe take a little sip, when things aren't going well, to remind you that good things can happen, too.

Somewhere, once, I read that there were actually tears of happiness. I hadn't had any of those, yet. I imagined they were like tiny jewels, liquid diamonds. They'd run down your cheeks very very slowly, one at a time. Like the tears of one of those crying Madonnas that Catholics like so much. I couldn't quite imagine it. Maybe they tasted really lovely, when they reached your lips and you could lick them off. Maybe they tasted like the most delicious sweets, but with a very delicate flavour. Like the smell of lilies, maybe, or pansies.

I weighed myself again, on New Year's Day. I'd lost another four pounds.

I got out a calendar of the year ahead and figured out that if I kept this blubbing diet up I'd be my target weight by Easter.

But long before Easter came, after they had the court case for my stealing Tarik, to which I pleaded guilty—I don't want to say anything about that, it was too horrible—I started having visits from someone I never expected to see again. The Lady with the Sash, from the cathedral.

When she came to visit, the first time, with the head of the Unit to introduce her, she spoke very little. She'd probably been told to keep quiet. She said her name was Rosemary. She gave me a little life story—only child like me, but from a posh family, never married so no children, aged 57, churchgoer (of course), and part-time librarian. Oh, and she had three male Siamese cats. She'd called them after angels. Raphael, Gabriel, Michael.

She was very careful to ask my permission to visit. She said it was part of something called a befriending scheme, for visiting kids like me.

'Like me? Losers with no friends, you mean. Thanks a lot,' I said, but it was true. Then I asked her the important question. 'But why me?'

'I remember you. The little lonely girl who used to come to the cathedral and sit by herself near the font, and never speak. I was worried about you, even then. When you ran away the first time, and stayed in the cathedral, we were in touch with the Social Services people to check how you were, where you lived. I . . . er . . . I meant to visit you in the Home . . . but . . . ' Her voice was posh but uncertain of itself, hesitant. It trailed off.

'But I stole Tarik and they put me here in the Unit,' I said.

'Then I heard of the befriending scheme and thought perhaps you might like a visit, now and then.' She looked anxiously at me through her big plastic-framed glasses. Her hair was neatly permed as usual, she wore a safe little cardigan, navy blue, with a pearl necklace. She had a sensible shiny black leather handbag, sensible brown shoes—the sort with little leather tassels on the front—and her usual tartan skirt with the big safety pin at the side. Fashionable she wasn't. She was a relic. I'd seen pictures of people like her, in a book about the 1940s. That was when she would have been little. It was like she was stuck in time.

'OK then, you can stay for a while,' I said, and the head of the Unit left the interview room.

There was an awkward silence.

'I suppose the Dog Whipper sent you,' I suddenly said, suspicious that Rosemary wasn't telling me the truth.

'The Dog Whipper, dear? There's been no dog whipper in the cathedral for hundreds of years, now.'

You know how it is when you are trying to see if someone is telling the truth or not? It can be a problem. Maddie, for instance. You just can't tell, sometimes. But with Rosemary I could see that she was telling the truth. She just wouldn't know how to tell a lie. She'd blush, or stammer, or something, if she tried.

She knew nothing, so I decided not to tell her anything about the Dog Whipper, or St Sidwell, or the fourteen angels, or Matthew Godwin the Master of the Music, the acrobatic monk, the Green Man. It was her bad luck if she couldn't see them and talk to them the same way I could.

'Of course. No Dog Whipper. So, how often are you planning to visit?'

'Once a week?' Again, there was that anxious look. I realized that she didn't really know how to talk to me. She was nervous of my reputation, I suppose. I imagine that the shrinks had been telling her what a nutcase I was. Suddenly I felt a little bit sorry for her. She was being brave, and finding it hard.

'We could give it a try,' I said, rather grumpy. I hadn't anything to lose.

So that's how it began. I suppose you could call it a friendship. I don't know much about friendship. There's this thing called trust, between friends, and trust and I hadn't been introduced, yet. Rosemary was more like an auntie, than a friend, really. An old spinster, totally uncool. Who'd have thought it? But I grew to like her.

Somewhere along the line, she had learned to listen. She just sat there, in the interview room with its oak floor and pine walls, two metal chairs and a stained coffee table, for an hour and a half every week, and listened. She never once made a face when I told her the worst bits. She never once offered advice, hardly ever interrupted, hardly ever asked too many questions.

I'd decided there was no point in telling her about the ghosts. She wouldn't understand. But I told her about all the nightmares I kept having. I wrote them down in my diary, and told them to her. Sometimes I pretended the ghosts were in dreams—like the ghosts of the quarriers, who still kept coming to threaten me by standing round my bedside, with the gloomy eyeless faces and their smell of cold damp.

She pursed her lips, nodded her head, and said she would try to think of how to get rid of them. It was like I had given her some difficult homework to do. It was fun, being the teacher, and her the schoolgirl. I didn't truly believe she could pass the test, and was quite looking forward to giving her a bad mark. I'd enjoy telling her to pull her faded old socks up.

Fifteen

A week later, Rosemary came into the interview room looking a bit excited. She was breathing heavier than usual, and put a finger to her lips, and kept glancing from side to side, as if I should keep a secret. She was carrying a white plastic supermarket bag, and inside it there was a cube. I could make out the shape of it, and thought she had brought me a present. She waited for the screw to go out of the room.

Then she unpacked the bag. There was a decorated cardboard box inside, about as big as a shoe box. I grabbed it and opened the lid, thinking there was something inside for me. It was empty.

'It's for your nightmares. We'll catch them in there and then I can take them away with me and get rid of them,' Rosemary said, going pink. I could tell she was thinking I would laugh at her.

I examined the box, instead. She'd taken lots of care. Down each edge she'd stuck silver tape with a green leaf design on it, and painted the brown cardboard a different colour on each of the six sides—'Red, orange, yellow, green, blue, indigo outside, and with violet inside, the colours of the rainbow,' she explained, with a nervous little laugh. I looked inside. It was lined with lovely velvet, the colour of violets, my favourite flowers. They grew in the banks beneath the hedges around here.

She'd decorated each panel, using a tiny paintbrush. There were foxgloves, marigolds, hyacinths, daffodils, daisies. They were quite good likenesses. In the centre of the lid flap, she'd made a perfectly circular hole, about a centimetre wide, big enough to get one finger in.

'That's for the nightmares to enter, you see,' she said.

I must have looked puzzled.

'Nightmares are rather stupid, but curious, too. If they see a hole, they have to go and look inside it,' she said. 'Then, when they are inside, we just cork them in, like this . . . ' and she produced from her handbag a small, red, rubber stopper, and shoved it in the hole. 'There!'

'But how do we get them in the hole?' I asked.

'You must put the box under your bed at night, and before you go to sleep you just ask for any nightmares to go and look there,' she said.

I thought this would never work and that she was a silly old bat, but didn't say so.

That night, I did as she said. I put the box under the bed, and kept the red rubber stopper under my pillow.

'Bad dreams, if you come in the night,

Look under my bed.

Instead of giving me a fright,

Go in the box, instead,' I muttered, a bit embarrassed. Rosemary had asked me to make up a rhyming prayer, and this was as good as I could do. Then I fell asleep.

There were three nightmares, all of them familiar.

The first one was of Saint Sidwell. In the dream, she came floating down from the east window of the cathedral, like she had done the night I slept there. She was like before, and if she stood sideways you couldn't see her. She was friendly and protective, like before, the big sister I never had. But now, the scar in her neck where she had been murdered, sliced with her own scythe, was open instead of being healed up. Blood was flowing from her neck, torrents of it, down her nice purple gown, spoiling it, and then over the floor.

Instead of a spring of water flowing from the ground where she'd been killed, there was a spring of sticky blood. Saint Sidwell was silent, appealing to me with her big eyes, as if I could rescue her. But, like in some of my worst nightmares, I couldn't move. I was frozen, watching the blood. I woke up, shaking.

In the second nightmare, all the bones of all the people who had ever been buried in the Close outside the cathedral came back to life. There were thousands of them rising out of the ground, and their bones made a horrible clicking, rattling noise, like dry sticks. They danced, fast and faster. There was fast music playing—a polka, I think.

Then a funny thing happened. They were all sucked together, like a giant vacuum cleaner had got them, and it turned them into one dead body, a giant one. It was a body so big and blubbery that it stretched from one end of the Close to the other, longer than the cathedral. I could see in the gloom that it was the body of a woman, naked. I looked from where I was standing on the top of the cathedral. Each of her feet was as big as a cottage, her huge hips were each the size of a blue whale, her stomach bigger than a hot air balloon, her boobs each the size of a haystack. Then I stared at her face and nearly fell off the cathedral.

It was my mother. And then, as I recognized her, I was sucked down from my perch, not flying, exactly, but falling towards the giant body, and then I was sucked inside her, through her navel. I was trapped inside my mother's body! Also, which was almost worse, I was going to grow into the body of my mother!

I couldn't breathe at all. It was airless and smelt of nail polish in there, like the sweets my mum once had which were meant to make your breath smell nice. I woke up, almost screaming.

The third nightmare was the most familiar one. It was just the old one of the quarriers in the cave where the stone for the cathedral came from, staring at me through their sunken, sightless eyes. There was an overpowering silence, and a smell of stale male sweat. Like the blind man, a friend of my mum's, who used to undress me when I was five or six, and give me a bath, with her watching—then he'd touch me, where he shouldn't, when she wasn't in the room. Again I woke, and looked at my watch. It was four thirty in the morning, and black outside.

I remembered the red rubber cork under my pillow, reached for it, found the cardboard box and jammed the cork into the hole in the lid. Then I managed to get some kip, but not much, for the rest of the night.

The next day, I was surprised to find that Rosemary was back to see me. She only came once a week, usually.

'Have you got the box?' she asked, whispering in case anyone heard.

'Of course. I had three nightmares last night . . . ' I started to say.

'Three? That's very good going, dear. But did you put the cork in?'

'Of course I did,' I said.

'Excellent. Give me the box at once.' She was breathing heavily, and shaking a bit.

I went back to my room and found it, where I'd left it in the cupboard, so that it was safe.

I shook the box, just to see if the nightmares made any sound. I half expected to hear them rattling round inside, but there was nothing. I handed it to Rosemary.

'Where are you going to open the box?' I asked.

'I'm not quite sure, yet. But don't worry, it will be far away. Somewhere by the sea, maybe . . . or the moors.'

Well, that night, the nightmares came back. Exactly the same ones, in the same order. *So much for Rosemary's well-meaning ideas*, I thought.

The first thing I told her, when she came on her weekly visit in six days' time, was that I'd had the worst week for nightmares in my whole life. I suppose I made a big fuss about it, just to show her that her box wasn't working. She was failing the test, and soon I'd be able to punish her.

She looked really surprised and upset. She'd brought the box back with her, and the red rubber stopper. I took it and opened the lid and shook the box out, upside down. I half expected the nightmares to drop out. But there was nothing, of course.

'Are you sure you said the prayer, beforehand?' she asked.

'Bad dreams, if you come in the night,
·Look under my bed.
Instead of giving me a fright,
Go in the box, instead,' I said.

'Mmm,' she said, thinking hard and blinking behind her big plastic spectacles, so that she looked like an owl with a perm. 'Maybe we have to give them an extra incentive to get inside the box.'

'How?'

'I'm trying to think how. What would you be curious about, if you were a nightmare? What would lure you through the hole?'

I thought hard, too. There was no sound in the interview room. We just sat and thought.

'I'm not too sure, but if I were a nightmare, I think I'd like to know how the sleeping person saw me. It's like, if I were a ghost, I'd want to be sure that I was recognized, and not invisible,' I said, thinking of the Dog Whipper, who was my secret ghost, thinking of the way Saint Sidwell disappeared, if you weren't directly in front of her.

'So. I've got it,' Rosemary suddenly said. 'You must draw little pictures of the nightmares, portraits of them, and put them inside the box, before you go to sleep. They won't be able to resist having a look, then.'

So that is what I did. I got my best felt-tips and some good paper. I drew a picture of Saint Sidwell with all the blood coming from her neck and flowing across the cathedral floor.

Then I drew the bones turning into my mother, and my mother lying across the Close, and me falling from the cathedral roof, and falling inside her. I drew it like a cartoon strip, in frames.

Last of all, using the black and the brown felt-tip, I just drew lots of tiny sightless men's eyes, without faces, and cut round them with my scissors and placed them in the box, on the velvet. So now it was a box with eyes and blood and bones in it. Then I shut the lid, but made sure to leave the round hole open. I put the box under my bed, said my little prayer again and went to sleep.

Same three nightmares, in the same order. I jammed the red rubber stopper on the box at four in the morning and managed to go back to sleep.

Next morning, Rosemary took the box away with her. She said she was going to the highest place on the moors, and was going to throw the nightmares to the west wind, as the clock struck twelve midday.

That night, for the first time in a month, I had no bad dreams. I woke in the morning and thought there was something wrong with me, as if there were something important missing, because I had grown so used to them.

I kept smiling and humming to myself over breakfast, and the other kids in the Secure Unit, who were used to me scowling all the time, kept glancing at each other nervously, as if I were a complete stranger who'd come to live with them.

Sixteen

Of course, I kept the little green leaf the Green Man had given me. I'd wrapped it in cotton wool, then put it inside a small plastic bag and stored it in my dream box. Sometimes I checked. The leaf was unchanged. It only went brown when the Dog Whipper was about to turn up again. When he was far away, it stayed green. As the weeks, then months, went by, I began to think I would never see the Dog Whipper again. I tried to forget him, but I couldn't.

I wasn't having the nightmares any more. Rosemary used to come each week, and tell me things from the outside world. She was the only regular visitor I had. I'd have a laugh with her, especially when she told me about all the goings-on at the church she went to, all the scandals about the vicar's moth-eaten trousers, the assistant priest's pet parrot which had learned some new swear words, the new woman preacher who nobody liked, because she looked like an alien, with big staring eyes and powdery skin.

It was a different world, hearing about Rosemary's posh friends and her posh childhood. She too was a single child. She told me about being sent to a private boarding school, which didn't sound much fun—all starched uniforms, hockey, and prefects who were allowed to bully you. We kind of agreed, without saying it in so many words, that childhood was 'not an entirely pleasant experience', as Rosemary would say.

Rosemary would get quite excited about the latest cathedral fund-raising effort—they were always trying to raise money. They were doing a sponsored walk to Canterbury. Someone was going to carry a cross—only it wasn't heavy, but a hollow one, made out of plastic, made to look like wood.

'That is so, so sad and boring!' I'd say, and giggle.

Rosemary just smiled and didn't seem to mind. Lately, she'd taken to wearing hats. She came in a knitted pink one, all covered in bobbles, with a purple ribbon, which I said was the ugliest thing I'd ever seen, then in a cream, straw one with a wide brim which she turned over at a jaunty angle so that she looked like a sailor in a sou'wester. I quite liked that one, and she was pleased.

One day, she and the Link Worker, who I hadn't seen for weeks, came at the same time. I could see that they were up to something. I got the warning signals. They had a plan for me.

'Now that you aren't getting the nightmares, and are so much slimmer and healthier, and things are so much better, we were wondering if you would like some more professional help,' Rosemary said, slightly apologetically. 'Only a little bit, Bella. Only if you want to.'

'What sort of professional help? Medical? Money advice? A barrister?' I said, just to tease her.

'There's a new child psychotherapist, from the clinic. She's wonderful,' the Link Worker chipped in.

I glared, and looked fierce under my knotted eyebrows, like I used to rehearse my hard look in the mirror, but agreed. I felt strong enough now. So the shrink came each week for two hours, on a Wednesday morning. We talked about everything—mostly about my mum—and she didn't smile too much or look jolly, like some of the others had done. She was quite small and ugly, with dark curly hair, and a snub nose, slightly yellow skin, with lots of moles. She used to sit opposite me and pull her knees up under her big baggy jersey and hug them, like she was comforting herself, and I realized that I was bigger than her, and better looking. Somehow, that helped me talk some more.

I told her about the time I found my mum lying on the kitchen floor when I came home from school, when I was about six or seven. There was an empty bottle of pills, an empty bottle of gin, and a note in red biro to me saying SORRY in big letters, which I could just about read. I called the ambulance. She got better.

'She hadn't taken the pills or drunk the gin, you know,' the shrink said, looking up the notes.

I'd been told this before. 'But why did she pretend?' I asked. So then we talked about that.

I told her about the time, one weekend, when I'd found my mum locked in the lavatory. I'd had to break the door down when I heard a gurgling noise. She was frothing at the mouth, horrible white stuff oozing down her chin. There was an empty bottle of bleach beside her.

'She'd taken bicarbonate of soda—harmless. She'd tipped the bleach down the sink,' the shrink said. 'It's part of her condition. Extreme attention seeking, to the extent of feigning all sorts of injury.' So then we talked about *that*.

We talked about everything. Sex. Drugs. Rock 'n' Roll. The Meaning of Life. Except I never mentioned the Dog Whipper or the other people and animals in the cathedral, or the quarriers. My visions.

It was the first time I'd done all the talking as one complete package. Things joined up, tied together. I didn't really understand it much better, but now at least I didn't think there was anything poisonous left inside me to say.

So that's how the months passed. The trouble was, I was getting to quite like the Secure Unit. I liked the routine, and the way everything was done for you. They said I was getting 'institutionalized'. I liked my room, and some of the teachers in the education block were OK. I was reading lots, and doing writing, too. One of the teachers said I was talented.

I'd been there almost a year. It was coming up to Christmas again. The season of goodwill, ha ha, very merry. Then they chucked me out. They said I was on the way to being cured. There was pressure for places, it was costing too much, all the usual excuses. I tried not to feel abandoned.

They found a different place for me, in the city. A Special Unit. Not a Secure Unit. The difference was, there were no high protective walls, no panic buttons. I was 'on licence'. I had to keep seeing the shrink, and the Link Worker, and there were places I wasn't allowed to visit, including going anywhere near the old Children's Home, or Tina and Tarik.

They didn't say that people from the Home couldn't visit me. I telephoned Maddie. She didn't seem keen, but she came over. When the staff said I had a visitor, I ran to the front door and hugged her—I'd never done this before, and she looked shocked—and then I saw she had brought Anthony with her, as some kind of protection I suppose. We all stared at each other, noticing how we had grown.

So I hugged him, as well. He looked even more shocked than Maddie.

'God, Bella, I don't believe it, you've got thin!' he said.

'I'm not thin and never will be. But I'm not fat, either,' I said. But he was. Taller, but fat as a barrel. There used to be books about a boy at public school called Billy Bunter. He was fat. Anthony looked like him, especially as he now wore glasses, black round ones, like Billy Bunter's. They magnified his yellow eyelashes.

Maddie had different coloured hair—very fair, almost white now, not brown—and it was cut shorter. She was wearing a mini-skirt, showing off her nice long legs, and was smoking a roll-up. She was sixteen now, and about to leave Care.

We stood there on the steps of the Special Unit, not quite knowing what to say to each other.

'It's been a long time,' I said.

'Almost a year, now,' said Maddie, puffing nervously. I wondered what she'd been told about me.

'How's Tina . . . and Tarik?' I said.

'She doesn't work at the Home any more,' Maddie said.

'Oh. I see.' I was disappointed. I wanted news.

'But I saw her a few weeks ago, in the village. She had Tarik with her,' said Anthony.

'How were they?' I had to know. I wanted to think they were OK.

'OK. They were OK.'

'How could you tell?'

'Well, I stopped and we talked and she said she was OK, that's how I know. She smiled and looked happy. She said she had a new job, in a factory, now that Tarik was going to nursery full-time. She's gutting chickens. Lovely job. How disgusting. I've gone vegetarian,' Anthony said.

His new diet hadn't helped him lose weight, I thought, but didn't say so.

'Did she say anything about Tarik?'

'She said he was—what was it?—a right little bundle of mischief. That was her exact expression. A right little bundle of mischief.'

'Interested in babies are you, still, Bella?' Maddie said. She chucked her cigarette on the pavement and ground it out with her shoe. 'Planning to have one soon, are you?' She laughed, not very pleasantly.

'Me? Not likely,' I said. 'How about you?'

'Accidents do happen,' she said, and leered at me. I wanted to tell her to be careful, that looking after a baby wasn't easy. But she wouldn't have listened.

I asked them in. The Special Unit was just an old house, nothing special to look at at all, really, despite its name.

'Not as posh as our place,' said Anthony.

'But the food's lots better,' I said, and exaggerated. I wasn't going to have him think he was in a better situation than me. 'More freedom too.'

It was true. My new Unit mostly had older children in it—right up to the age of seventeen. They could come and go as they liked, the ones who were working or at college. They'd all had mental problems. I was the youngest. It was nice to get away from little kids, I said to Maddie. 'Are they still a pain?'

She nodded. 'Yup.'

'Do you remember the tricks we played on them?' I asked.

She said she did, but she sounded a bit bored. She sat there without saying anything while Anthony and I went over every detail of the horrible things we had done to the younger kids.

'Remember the time we got that ants' nest and put it in the bed of the girl at the end of the corridor, the one who looked like a rat—what was her name?' I said.

'Yes,' he said, dreamily. 'Remember the time we got that yellow emulsion paint and put it in a saucepan and warmed it up and told one of them it was lovely custard?' he said. 'All over that apple pie, and he said yum yum and ate it up.'

'The itching powder. The fart cushion. The fake dog poo. The plastic vomit, with its little bits of sweetcorn, very realistic. But you could buy all those, from a joke shop. Our home-made tricks were best,' I said.

'The metal door handle we wired up to the mains so that you got an electric shock. The fishing line we rigged up between the trees, as a trip wire—very effective,' Anthony sighed.

'Remember the time we made a horrible wrinkly hand, out of plasticine, a giant one with warts on it, and black hair growing from them, and then we put it on a bamboo pole and made it scratch at the bedroom window of that girl with the plaits?'

'With its bright red finger nails? Yes, I remember. She peed in her bed for a week!' he said, happily. 'Those were the days, Bella.'

'Sods, weren't we?' I said.

'Little fat sods,' he said. He kept looking at me and I knew that he was thinking that we couldn't ever be friends again, now that I wasn't so fat.

'No more Big Three,' I said. Maddie looked as if she didn't know what I was talking about.

Sometimes people split apart. A year's an awfully long time, when you are young.

Seventeen

One day I looked in my cupboard for the dream box, with its pretty flower designs made by Rosemary, and its purple lining. I know the exact date I did this, because I wrote it in my diary. It was December 11th. I took out the plastic bag with my green leaf in it, unwrapped it—and it had turned brown.

The Dog Whipper was calling me, after months and months of silence! My mouth went dry, my heart started doing a double-beat, bim-bam, bim-bam, high in my chest. I grabbed my warmest fleece, shoved it on, and a coat and a deeply unfashionable woolly hat, because the weather had been frosty overnight. I walked into the centre of the city, as fast as I could.

It was the first time in ages that I'd been back to the cathedral. I hoped Rosemary wouldn't be on duty. She wasn't. I went to my old place, near the font, and sat on a pew and waited. And waited and waited.

In the old days, I used to say I wasn't frightened of anything, except snakes. The dark, spiders, heights, small spaces, horror films—nothing bothered me. I'd had so much to be frightened of, when I was little, that all the fear had been used up. But, nowadays, I was easily nervous. I looked around, and shivered. I'm not sure what I was afraid of. The unknown, I suppose. I wasn't sure what was going to happen. My skin prickled. I shivered. My teeth began to chatter, until I tightened my jaw. I shut my eyes, but that didn't help. I clutched my arms around me, and held on.

I must have been there an hour, and was getting cold, when I saw him. He was down past the big organ pipes reaching to the ceiling, past the old gold and blue clock, past the medieval animal carvings, past the tombs of the bishops who had died hundreds of years ago.' He was beckoning. Standing there in a quiet corner in his long black cape, with its hood up, so that I couldn't see his eyes, but I knew it was him.

I walked as quickly as I could down the aisle. There was nobody else near—just me and the Dog Whipper. He held out a hand and now I could see his eyes, kind and patient, under his hood.

'Bella. Bella. Now, your name really does mean what it does in Italian. Beautiful,' he said, in his teasing voice.

'Don't be so silly. Just because I've lost some weight,' I said. I was so pleased to see him that I had started crying, and he fetched a big clean perfectly white handkerchief from a pocket in his cape and handed it to me. I stood there, blubbing. The handkerchief smelt of mint, somehow.

'It is because you are beautiful inside. Your internal beauty has come to the surface,' he said, still teasing.

'Don't be so stupid. You talk rubbish, like you always did,' I said, and punched him lightly on his shoulder, but I liked his idea very much.

'I have been thinking how you have changed, and the progress you have been making,' he said. He had sat down on a stone seat, and I sat too, still clutching his hand.

'How did you know? Did Rosemary . . . ?'

'No. Rosemary and I do not communicate. She cannot see me. You understand that, don't you? No, the leaf the

Green Man gave you is my connection to you, and through it I knew how things were with you. But I did not get in touch before because you were doing so well without me—and I have so many others to attend to, you know.'

'So, why now?' I asked.

'Once, you told me what your greatest wish would be. I could not do anything about it then, but now . . . '

I tried to remember. I wiped my tears away, put his handkerchief in my pocket, and thought hard for a minute. I couldn't think what it was I had wished for.

'Come with me,' he said, and he led me down to the very far end of the cathedral, where there's a chapel lit by a lot of candles. People leave messages there, and prayers—things they wish for. I used to read them. Often, the messages would be about people who are ill, and would hope they'd get better.

There was no one in there, in the half dark, except for a single figure, a woman, praying on her knees, all by herself. Even from behind, which is where I viewed her from, I knew who it was.

It was my mother.

I stood there, staring. I forgot to breathe. Everything had changed. My mother would never have prayed, in the old days. I had not seen her for about three years. She looked so much older.

I had to sit down, because my legs went weak. It was the first time this had happened to me. I thought I was going to faint, and had to put my head between my knees for a moment. My brow felt all clammy, and I felt like I was maybe going to be sick.

Her hair was grey, now. She was only forty, but her hair was fully grey. She seemed smaller, too—or was it that I was bigger? I sat there only for a second or two, taking this in, then I ran to her. She heard me coming, and turned, and I saw her face.

So familiar, but so strange to me. I couldn't tell what had changed. She smiled, held out her arms, still on her knees, and as I bent down to kiss her she said, 'The power of prayer. My prayers have been answered.'

Then she hugged me, a fierce, strong hug, pulling me down to her level, not rising to mine, so that I too was on my knees and there we were, mother and daughter, both on our knees in the chapel.

'Pray with me,' she said, letting go and putting her hands together, facing the altar. I couldn't pray. I didn't know how to. No one had ever taught me. But I went through the motions. I put my hands together, and closed my eyes, but every couple of seconds I glanced sideways at her to check that she was still there, to check that this was really happening.

I could see her lips moving silently. She was talking to somebody, giving thanks. I suppose it must have been a saint or Jesus she was talking to, or God. All I knew was that my mother was back.

Then I was aware of the Dog Whipper coming up behind me. He always knew when I was being truthful. He knew that I wasn't really praying, and that I was stuck. I looked at him for help. He smiled quietly and held out a hand, palm down, just to say that it would be all right, and to relax.

We were like that, my mother and me, for what seemed ages. Then, with my knees beginning to hurt, she rose and, when I stood up, I could tell that I was now much taller than her.

'My Bella. My child,' was all she said at first, over and over again. Then she asked me to forgive her. She gripped my hands hard in hers and came closer, so that her face was only inches from mine and I was staring down into her eyes. It made such a difference, staring down at her, rather than up.

She wore no mascara or eye-liner. I was lost in her eyes, which looked somehow different from before, but I couldn't spot the difference, yet. It was like drowning in a big lake.

'Forgive me,' she said. She didn't plead with me, or command me to forgive her. She just said it kind of flat, as if she had rehearsed it.

'Of course,' I said. The child always forgives its mother, or wants to.

Only when I said the words could I escape her eyes, and look over her shoulder, at all the pretty candles, the stained glass in the bleak wintry sunlight, the creamy coloured stonework, and my eyes went up to the vaults above.

I could feel all my old friends in the cathedral were somehow with me, watching over me. The Green Man, with his big laugh and hair made of roots and branches. The tumbling monk, standing on his hands so that his brown cassock fell down, but luckily he was wearing underpants, also brown. St Sidwell, with her beautiful purple robes and little golden scythe. The patient mother pig, carved from stone, with her snorting, suckling piglets. The elephant carved from wood, with the feet of a cow, and two sets of ears. All the dead bishops. Matthew Godwin, the child genius composer—even he was looking kindly at me, not grumpy like he used to be.

The fourteen angels with their musical instruments were there, and in my imagination they started to play so that the air was filled with wonderful music, but my mother couldn't hear it. She was not one of us.

Then I suddenly realized that she couldn't see the Dog Whipper, either. He was standing there, right next to us, and only I could see him. Yet it was he who had brought her to the cathedral, I knew.

'How did you find me? How did you know where to come?' I said.

'I knew you were in this city somewhere. I thought that if I came to the cathedral, and prayed, I would find you,' she said.

'So—have you been here before? Do you recognize this place, and the people who are here?' I asked.

It was my way of double checking that she couldn't see the Dog Whipper.

'No. I've never been here before. Very nice, isn't it?' she said. 'Very peaceful. Ever so old.'

Nice? Nice? I thought. *Is that all she can say?* And I didn't like the word peaceful, either. That was what a lot of people wrote in the Visitors Book. To me the cathedral was exciting, mysterious, dangerous, even. Not peaceful.

This was my special, magic place and she called it nice. Like a nice cup of tea, one of her favourite things in life. The Dog Whipper was standing back, and when I looked at him he smiled and shrugged his shoulders as if to say, some of us have got it, some of us haven't. You win some, you lose some.

I began to feel that something was missing. I was expecting my mother to say all sorts of things about me and to me—like, how I'd grown, how I was no longer so fat, and I thought she'd be wanting to find out things about me, like my education and friends and where I was living and how the care authorities were treating me. She had battled with them to keep me—court case after court case. I could remember them, and being questioned by all sorts of social workers and guardians *ad litam* about where I wanted to live, and me saying that I still wanted to live with my mum—which I couldn't help wanting, in spite of everything she had done—and that I still wanted that, because she was still my mum and had some kind of home she could offer me, not like my dad, who was in jail.

But they still took me away from her, and told me it wouldn't be good for me to see her.

So I thought that at least she'd try to update herself on my situation. But she didn't.

She walked down the aisle of the cathedral towards the entrance and she started telling me about what a difficult journey she had had, how the train was late, how expensive it was, how much the taxi had charged her to get to the cathedral from the station, the terrible price of a sandwich she had eaten . . . the weather on her journey, as if I might be in the least bit interested in the weather, and my heart sank.

I was part of her world again. Or, like, left outside it, looking in, like a doll left out in the rain. I felt shrunk, and made invisible, like the so-called ghosts. Like I used to feel in the Children's Home. There are lots of ways of being invisible, or being made invisible. I was just a ghost to her. Not the real me.

I could feel all my friends in the cathedral wishing me good luck, and the angels started playing some new music. It made me want to dance, but I couldn't, not with my mother there. The tumbler turned cartwheels faster and faster, as if to make me smile, and the Green Man waved his branches about, which made swooshing noises, and one branch came down quite low, as if to offer to pick me up and take me to safety, and I heard his voice, like the wind, but I knew I had to be with my mum.

The Dog Whipper, who was the only one of the so-called ghosts allowed to leave the cathedral, followed us out into the cold sunshine, across the Close. I knew that he was there to look after me. I guessed I might still need him.

He had brought her here—even if she didn't know it. He was following up, to see what would happen next, now that my biggest wish had been granted. Suddenly, it all seemed like a big test of me, and I wanted to run away.

I clutched the big, clean, white handkerchief he had given me, and hoped it would bring me luck.

Eighteen

I tried hard for my mother, I really tried. I did everything she wanted, I listened to her endless complaints, I followed where she went.

Her first stop was to a chemist's shop, to pick up a prescription. She was on three kinds of medicine. 'My pink ones, my little green ones, and these big red and black ones,' she said, pointing out each kind of pill. She kept them in a round, white, plastic dispenser which had sixteen little compartments, one for every waking hour of the day.

On each compartment she'd written in tiny letters with an indelible biro the hour she needed to take the pills, starting at eight in the morning after she woke and finishing at midnight, before sleep.

'I'd be lost without my little white box. Mother's little helpers, these pills are,' she said, and laughed, very bright-eyed. I could see what was different about her face, now. In the past, her eyes, which are bluey-green, were very distant and dull—kind of misted over, almost. Now, her eyes shone brightly and she fixed them on me all the while, too much, so I wanted to look away and hide. It was almost like her eyes were alight with blue flames. She was always checking me out. Except that I could see that, deep down, she was more interested in her pills than in me.

She wasn't checking me out to see who I was. She was checking me out to see how her new act was going down. I was her audience. She still hadn't asked me anything, so I thought I'd tell her, anyway, to balance things up.

'Don't you notice how much weight I've lost, Mum?' I asked.

'Have you, darling?' she said blankly, peering at me and looking puzzled.

I told her about all the trouble I had been in. How I had stolen Tarik, and the court case afterwards, and the Secure Unit. I guess she knew all about it already, because my Link Worker said she'd been informed, through the courts. But she just sounded very vague and kept saying things like 'You shouldn't have done that', 'May the Lord forgive you', and 'What a wicked girl', but without any feeling in her voice, as if she wasn't really interested.

I wanted to shock her, then. I wanted to be really nasty.

'Mum, why did they let you out of hospital? Couldn't they do any more for you?' I said in as cold a tone as I could make.

Her voice perked up, now we were talking about her again, not me.

'Quite the opposite, darling. They found these new pills for me, and said I could go. It was a year ago, they let me out.'

I thought how strange this was. It was a year ago that they had locked me up. One out, one in.

'Why didn't you come before?'

She didn't answer, like she hadn't heard the question. I remembered this old trick of hers.

Instead, she started blabbing about the little flat they had found her—'Sheltered accommodation. A nice quiet street, in a cul-de-sac. There's a warden. She understands me. We're allowed visitors. You must come up and see me.' Blab, blab, blab.

'What sort of visitors?' I asked.

'Well, there's my sister, your aunt Zara.' I remembered Zara, of course. Everything had gone right for Zara—good job, husband, three nice children, no trouble.

'And then there's Pat.'

'Who's Pat?' I didn't know if Pat was male or female.

'My new boyfriend. I met him in the hospital. He's nice, with nice soft hands. He's an undertaker. Ever so gentle. You'd like him, Bella.'

I knew at once I wouldn't. I added undertakers to my list of new things to be afraid of. I thought of his soft white hands handling corpses. Then I thought of them handling me in a way they shouldn't. The way two of her other boyfriends had done. The blind man, and the one who said he was a magician. He promised he'd show me tricks if I sat on his knee, which I foolishly did, being only five years old at the time.

We stayed there outside the chemist's shop, on a bench, while she arranged all her pills into their right compartments. I got the feeling it was an important thing for her to do, something she did every day. Her little ritual.

Then, when they were all packed away, she sighed happily and started telling me about how she had been converted to some kind of happy-clappy revivalist Christian sect called The Redeemed while she'd been in hospital, and how she loved it, singing and praying together every night in someone's home just around the corner from where she lived. She told me the names of each of the members—as if I were in the least bit interested—and a little story about each one, and how their lives had changed now they were redeemed, which took about an hour. I was totally bored, but did she notice? Of course not.

She had one of their glossy leaflets, which she made me take. It had a picture of a deer on it, and a rainbow sheltering a smiling child, and bright sunshine. Spare me, I thought.

'It's not like that cathedral. Rather dull in there, isn't it? Nice but dull. No, we're the new way. Charismatic. *We* have been redeemed.' She said the word in a kind of robot-like way, like she'd been brainwashed. I knew it wasn't going to be any good talking to her about it.

She was happy because she'd found something which meant she didn't have to ask herself any more difficult questions. Ever. But I was going to ask them for her.

'So . . . you haven't been ill lately then? No more ambulances rushing you to hospital? No more falling over in the street, in a fit, or bleeding to death. Or sicking your guts up or anything?' I said sarcastically.

'Oh, no. Whatever makes you ask that?' she said. The funny thing was, she looked genuinely surprised, as if I were talking about someone else.

'I remember when you said you were dying of cancer.'

'Me? Oh, no. You must have imagined it, Bella. You always did have a strong imagination.' She gave a tinkly little laugh, like a handbell ringing in an attic. I thought I was going mad, like before.

Later, we went for a walk in the park. A squirrel came up, looking for nuts. I like squirrels but my mum shied away.

'Tree rats. And they're covered in fleas, you know. Never touch a squirrel, Bella. You might catch something nasty,' she said. She listed all their diseases, in alphabetical order. I'd forgotten how much she knew about different kinds of diseases. She was like a walking medical dictionary. It made me anxious to listen to her.

We were sitting on the grass under a big tree. Something made me look across the park, to the far distance. There, by the red painted iron gates at the entrance, stood an old man. It was the Dog Whipper, in his disguise. He wore his boring brown trousers and turquoise parka, with the hood up, but I knew it was him. He was looking at us. I felt relieved. He must be keeping an eye on me, to see that I was OK. I wished he would come closer, so that I could ask him something. But he kept his distance.

We went to get an ice-cream. My mum had a strawberry one, and took her 'two o'clock in the afternoon' pills with it. I said I had to make a call on my mobile. 'Go ahead,' she said, without much interest.

'In private, Mum,' I said. She didn't seem to mind.

I walked away and dialled up Rosemary. I told her I was with my mum.

'Oh, how lovely for you. You must be happy. That was what you always wanted,' was the first thing she said. I could see that she hadn't thought it through.

'But you don't understand. That's why they put me in care. To keep me away from her,' I said. 'Will I get into trouble? I found her in the cathedral. She was praying. She's changed.'

'Praying? Changed? How wonderful,' Rosemary said. She still didn't get the point.

'No, no, no. It's not wonderful. She's joined some religious cult. The Redeemed. And she's on some new pills. Before, she was always far away and in her own head. You could never tell what was going on with her. Now, she doesn't stop talking about herself. She's in your face, and there's a horrible gleam in her eye. Can you imagine, blue eyes, but like they are on fire? A blue flame. It's scary. I preferred her the old way . . . ' I said, and started to sob.

'Oh, dear,' said Rosemary.

'What shall I do? Will I get into trouble for seeing her?'

'I don't know,' she said, which was honest, as usual. Then she said I would have to tell my Link Worker, and that the best thing was just to keep talking to my mother but to be ready to run away if she suggested anything strange or unusual.

'Do you want me to call the police?' she asked.

'Of course not. I can handle this,' I said, but I wasn't sure if I could.

When I went back to my mum, she had finished her ice-cream. There was a thick ring of pink around her lips, and a blob of ice-cream had dropped onto her blouse. I pointed them out but she didn't bother to clean herself up. She never used to be a messy eater. In fact, the opposite. She used to eat very carefully, and told me I had to chew my food twenty times before swallowing it. She used to count aloud while I did so. It was one of her rules. No wonder I used to gobble my food when they took me away from her.

She wasn't at all interested in who I had been ringing.

'How long are you here for?' I asked.

'Oh, only for the afternoon. I have to catch the three o'clock train back,' she said.

I looked at my watch. It was two thirty. We were a twenty minute walk from the station.

'But that means we'll only have another half an hour,' I said.

'Mm . . . I know. I mustn't forget my three o'clock pills. I think I will take them just before getting on the train, in case I forget,' she said.

I despaired, then. There was so much to talk about, and so little time, but she started on about the weather, and was worried that it might rain, but that she had brought her umbrella just in case, and her plastic mac, and how it rained quite a lot where she lived up north, but that her flat was very comfortable and that she had good neighbours, then she started telling me about each one, in turn, things she had told me only an hour or two ago. I wanted to scream. I had never met these people, and wasn't at all interested in them. What about *me*?

Then we left the park and walked to the station and she took her pills and got on the train.

She pecked me hard on the cheek. Her lips were the shape of a sharp beak. I could feel some of the strawberry ice-cream sticking to me. She gave me her telephone number and address, and told me to visit her, but didn't ask me for mine, so I didn't give it to her. She didn't say anything about coming down again.

'Pray every day for me, Bella,' were her last words.

She waved goodbye and I could see her framed in the train window, clutching her little white pill dispenser in one hand and one of the pamphlets from The Redeemed in the other one.

I thought I might never see her again, and that I didn't want to.

I cried into the Dog Whipper's minty white hanky on the way back to my Special Unit from the station.

But then, I cried easily these days. Buckets of tears.

Nineteen

I went through a bad patch, after that. I lost the plot, and went crazy for a week or two. I was more than one sandwich short of a picnic, for a while.

I trudged through the wet streets to the cathedral every day, looking for the Dog Whipper. Everyone was getting ready for Christmas, and for carol concerts, so the cathedral was busy. I saw the priests in their black floor-length skirts scurrying about. But no Dog Whipper.

None of my other old friends in the cathedral spoke to me—the Green Man, the angels, the acrobat monk, the various bishops, prophets, holy men, knights and their ladies, madonnas and saints. They were just in their usual places, silent, and looking like they must appear to everyone else. Just carvings, with no life. Dead wood. Stone dead. Something had changed.

It was as if the Dog Whipper had told them not to speak to me. He must know I was angry with him. He had arranged for me to meet my mother, my greatest wish, and she was such a disappointment to me. Of course I'd be cross with him. He must have known it wouldn't work out. He knew everything. So why had he done it? To teach me a lesson?

It was no good talking to Rosemary about it. She wouldn't understand. I thought of going to see the shrink, but then I thought she'd say I was mad, and lock me up again.

I sat in the cathedral, waiting. The Dog Whipper didn't come. So then I started to plan. I was going to give the Dog Whipper a test, a big test. I wanted to see him under pressure. I wanted to see if he would crack.

I got Anthony to help me. He was good with a computer, and a scanner. We used the ones in my Unit, when people were out.

We designed and printed 200 colour leaflets. It took us ages. There was a big picture of a mongrel, a stringy lurcher, brown and black. We put a big wooden cross next to it, and underneath in big letters **'Christmas Service for THE DOG, man's best friend. For his faithfulness. Bring your dog to the cathedral on December 22nd. A gift for each dog, plus wine and mince pies for the owners.'**

We were doing our tricks again. It was like the old days of the Big Three. Except, this time, Anthony was up for it, but Maddie wasn't interested. She said it was kids' games, and that she was too busy, seeing her new boyfriend, and getting ready to leave Care.

We went round to see the down-and-outs. We only gave leaflets to those who had dogs. We asked them to let their other friends with dogs know, and they said they would.

'The cathedral's never tried it before. They're not quite sure how many are coming, so they've got in extra wine, like on a sale or return basis. So there should be enough to go round—and lots of mince pies too, and loads of tins of dog food and collars and flea powder and vouchers for veterinary treatment and such . . . ' I told them in my poshest voice, letting my imagination run riot. I'd got myself a little silver cross, which I wore round my neck. I looked pious, part of the God Squad.

The beggars' eyes lit up. 'We'll be there, and all our mates,' they said.

On the big day, Anthony and I were waiting in the cathedral, watching. People with dogs started to arrive early. Dogs on strings, dogs on chains, dogs on leather leads, all sniffing and looking excited. It was going to be a canine carnival, they could tell.

There were dogs carrying sticks in their mouths. Slurping and drooling dogs. Then, as more arrived, there were barking dogs, of course. The first one to start was a small, intelligent black-and-tan mongrel terrier, who pranced up and down on her back legs.

A dirty black and white long-haired trotting dog, head held high, came in unaccompanied and started running about the aisles, sniffing all the other dogs' bottoms, and yelping with excitement.

Some country sheepdogs, allowed to roam, began to round up a bunch of timid city dogs, terrifying them. They cowered in one of the side chapels, like sheep in a pen. They howled, feeling sorry for themselves, getting their leads tangled up, tripping their owners.

That set off a red setter, one of the few pedigrees. He began to howl, and tried to break free from a stern woman with scraggy hair, dressed in leathers, like a motorcyclist. A tubby dog who weighed about twice what he should have done, with big paws and stubby legs, rolled on his back, showing all his large, wobbly private parts, and tripped up one of the priests, who had come hurrying down the aisle to see what all the bother was.

'Shut the doors, shut the doors! There's been some mistake,' he shouted from where he sprawled in the nave, but it was too late now. A crowd, each person with a dog, was pushing in. They had been drinking together and come as a gang.

'Where's the wine, father?' they asked. The priest looked blank. One man, with a completely shaven head but stubble all over his face, like a bog brush, held out the leaflet we had made. 'The wine,' he said, stabbing it with his finger.

One tattooed man wore a metal helmet, with cow horns sticking out of it. His skinny Goth girlfriend, with black hair, black eyes, and black lips, wore a leopardskin lycra suit, very tight. They had a black Alsatian each, his and hers. You wouldn't want to tangle with them—the couple, I mean; the dogs looked OK.

'And the prezzies for the dogs? Where are they?' said a trembling old lady dressed in Oxfam cast-offs. She had her little dog in a plastic carrier bag, its head popping out. It was tiny but hairy. You couldn't see its eyes for a long fringe. It was getting too excited, and yapping like a wound-up toy, hysterical.

Big dogs, small dogs, stray dogs, shy dogs, groomed dogs, dogs who had never seen a brush. Dogs with healthy wet noses, sniffing everything. Dogs with dried-up noses, looking miserable. Dog hair was drifting in the beams of weak winter sunlight coming in through the windows, and then settling along the aisles, a bit like snow.

Growl, yap, snap, whine, yelp, sniff, shiver, drool, bark went the dogs. Tug, tug went the owners, with their dog-leads. 'Sit! Down! Heel!' was what they shouted, but their dogs took no notice. It was all tails, teeth, and paws, and a hundred wet noses sniffed the air. It must have been dog heaven. All we needed now were bones to chew, and a warm fire to flop in front of.

I got down on all fours, and began to growl, to get the dogs even more excited. I could feel the cold stone flags on my hands and through my jeans, on my knees. I growled as deep as I could, and began to bark. Anthony moved away, pretending he wasn't with me.

I began to sniff, hard and urgently. If I couldn't be part of the world of the spirits, I wanted to be part of the world of the dog. I wanted to live in their smelly universe, I wanted to smell that beautiful poodle there, thirty yards away, and tell him from the Pekinese next to him. But I couldn't, because my nose wasn't up to it, not even when I wet it by spitting on my hand and rubbing the spit in.

But I could smell the general smell of wet dogs — musty, stale, slightly sweet, like the well-rotted compost the gardener used to make in my last Children's Home but one.

I lifted my hand to my face and looked at the dog hair it had picked up, on my palm. Individual hairs, quite fine, of brown, white, grey, and black. I wondered what a blanket made of dog hair would be like. I wanted to disappear under the fur of a dog. I stood up again. If only I could have been a dog. Life would have been a lot simpler.

The biggest dog was a deerhound, shaggy and wild, the colour of a peat bog. The smallest was one you could hold in one hand, or slip up the sleeve of your coat. When I went near it I could smell some horrible scent someone had smothered it in. I imagined what that did to its sensitive nose, poor thing.

Other human visitors to the cathedral grouped together, terrified, down one side, with the dog lot the other. The whole cathedral began to smell doggy. Dogs brought in not only their fusty smell with them, but lots of mud and drips, because it had been raining. One big one shook himself and the spray went everywhere, including over the black habits of a group of visiting nuns, who backed away, squealing, 'Protect us, Lord!'

One dog had been dressed up for Christmas, with a little red pointed hat on, and a red and white fur collar. There were no less than two three-legged dogs, and one completely blind one, who kept bumping into things.

The one I liked the most was a curly spaniel-type dog. He had a kind expression, and round his neck was a little plastic bucket for people to put coins in. I recognized him as the dog belonging to the down-and-out who always slept under one of the arches near the city walls.

By now, a big row was developing. People wanted freebies, and they weren't getting any. Anthony and I were giggling, and wondering what would happen next. I was waiting for the Dog Whipper.

Then I saw him. He came hurrying down the steps from his quarters high above the nave. Yes, he had his long dog-whipping stick with him. Yes, he was looking angry. This must be like the old days for him. I thought of pointing him out to Anthony, then knew that he wouldn't be able to see him.

Nor could all the dog-owners, nor the dogs, apparently. The Dog Whipper began to stride up and down between the rows of seats, waving his arms about, swishing his stick. No one took a bit of notice. I went up closer.

His pale white face had gone deep pink. Even the white flat patch on the end of his nose, like he was pushing it up against an invisible pane of glass, had gone pink. His eyes were staring about him, wildly.

'Be gone with you! Out, curs and wretches!' he shouted, using old-fashioned language. 'Get ye hence, avaunt!' Then he said things in a kind of French, I think. The more angry he became, the stranger his language. I couldn't understand. It was like he was using all his dog-chasing phrases from hundreds of years ago.

Then something unexpected happened. He sat down, and laughed.

He just collapsed on a wooden bench, and burst out laughing. Then he beckoned to me.

'It was never as bad as this! Even in the thirteenth century. You've done well, Bella. You've created a real riot. The worst yet.'

About a dozen of the dog-owners had cornered a priest, and were threatening him. Several of the sheepdogs had rounded up a group of German women tourists, and were barking at them. The tourists huddled together, trembling, like fat old ewes. Then they got on their mobile phones, ringing the police, the German Embassy, whoever they could get hold of.

'*Ja*, I am saying, I am in the cathedral. Bring guns, many guns!' one woman with flaxen hair and gold spectacles was screaming.

I could count ten pools of dog pee, and four piles of dog poop. It must have been the nervous tension which made the dogs want to go. Three of the volunteer helpers at the cathedral had climbed up the steps of the lectern, and there they clung to each other, like on a little island, while dogs yapped around them, patrolling like sharks who had scented blood.

Puppies raced happily round the pillars, playing chase. A very old Rottweiler had fallen asleep in the Bishop's Chair. There were four or five separate dog fights going on, quite nasty ones, with blood. The pit bull terriers were the worst. They wouldn't let go with their teeth.

I could hear the sound of the police sirens coming through the city traffic. Anthony and I gave each other high fives. This was our best trick yet.

Twenty

'A wonderful riot. More than I could ever cope with. I give up. How wonderful it is, to give up trying, sometimes, don't you think, Bella?' said the Dog Whipper. 'We'll leave it to the police, shall we?' He gave me a hug, my first ever from him.

'I don't think it's over, yet. We've got some uninvited guests. It's not just dogs,' I said, looking over his shoulder.

Streaming in through the cathedral doors was a flock of flying human bones—the ones which had been buried out in the Close for more than a thousand years.

I don't think any other person but me and the Dog Whipper could see them. But the dogs could. The sight— or smell, perhaps—of bones sent them even wilder. I don't know why people think old bones are white. Those are only the cleaned-up ones. These were faded yellow and brown ones. Some had bits of earth still clinging to them. They kept on coming through the wide-open doors. I could recognize leg-bones, shoulder-bones, hip-joints, elbows, knee-caps. Thousands of them, too many to count. And as they came, the noise from the dogs grew even louder. Some howled, some yapped, but most just barked with excitement. The few who were still half under the control of their owners broke free, and now there were a couple of hundred dogs chasing aerial bones.

They did it by leaping into the air and snapping. I never saw a single dog actually catch a bone. It was as if the bones were teasing them. I saw a Dobermann crouch on all four paws, sharp ears pricked up, watching three ribs float past. Then it sprang and snapped, drool flying from its chops. But the ribs just did a mid-air flip, and the dog snapped only air, which, of course, made it madder still. Its owner couldn't figure it out, and began to scream at it.

It looked as though the dogs had suddenly all lost their marbles together—like they all had rabies, or something. They were leaping into the air, climbing on the seats, scrambling up the walls. One little one, a Pekinese, somehow climbed up onto a screen near the organ, and launched itself into space, snapping wildly all the while. Luckily, its owner caught it, and got bitten for her trouble, because it just kept snapping at a delicious invisible bone which it could see but the owner couldn't.

Then, with the bones still flying around above our heads, I saw among them the brass eagle from the lectern—the place where the priests read the lesson. It had obviously grown fed up with standing still for centuries with its wings spread wide to support the Bible, and had flown free. It swooped up and down the cathedral, screeching.

This woke up the old owls carved in stone in one of the side chapels. They flew out together, hooting. This wakened the little carved dogs at the feet of various knights and ladies whose stone effigies lined the walls of the cathedral, so now we had a pack of ghost dogs mixing it with the real dogs and soon, as dogs do, they were fighting.

Watching the real dogs fighting the invisible dogs was even more puzzling to the owners than the sight of them snapping at invisible bones. One mastiff seized a ghost dog—a little terrier—by the throat and wrestled it to the ground. Its owner couldn't figure out what was going on at all.

All the other carved animals joined in—the pigs from the ceiling, the funny elephant with the feet of a cow and two sets of ears, knights' horses, and even a dragon or two. The one from the George and the Dragon boss about seventy feet above our heads came swooping down, flapping its bright green leathery wings, and started breathing fire at the dogs, who cowered in a corner, never having met a dragon before.

All the angels with their musical instruments joined in, and then a whole bunch of jesters—the ones carved on oak seats—started prancing about, banging their drums, sounding their horns, and generally having a riot.

Various Green Men wandered about, looking like trees, which was a mistake, because the dogs saw them, cocked their legs and peed all over their trunks, which made the Green Men cross, so they started kicking the dogs, so now we saw the occasional dog flying through the air from a well-aimed invisible kick—which mystified their owners even more.

Then the characters from the stained glass, and from the paintings, woke from their long sleep. Cherubs tooted on trumpets, a hundred miracles were performed in front of our eyes, prayers were prayed and songs sung, a lot of them in Latin, which I didn't understand. A couple of lions started prowling around, snarling and showing their fangs, having come to life from being locked in stone, and I hid behind the Dog Whipper, to protect me.

It was as if all of them were on their worst behaviour, like the Big Three, only more so. It was because they had grown so tired of being locked up as statues or glass windows or paintings, and wanted to be free again. Having been locked up myself, I knew how they felt. The dog invasion had woken them from their slumbers, and they were all wanting to have fun, while they could.

In one corner, from where a wonderful smell of hot spices was coming, a group of minstrels were sitting down to a medieval winter feast. They drank something made from honey which the Dog Whipper said was called mead. They slurped at a kind of thick barley soup, they tore meat with their bare teeth from cooked bones (which they threw to their ghost dogs), they belched and sang and shouted at each other as if there was no tomorrow. They were dressed in leather and colourful wool—the men up one end, the women at the other, with children, lots of them, all around.

It looked fun, to be a medieval child. For example, deodorants, toothbrushes, and Kate Bush hadn't yet been invented. School didn't yet exist—not for most children, anyway. I expect they had hardships. Saint Sidwell had told me of all the work they had to do, and all the dirt and disease, and the way they died so young, but I still thought their life looked good compared with mine.

But lurking around in the background were all the devils and evil spirits. I could see them in the dim shadows. There were the usual little red devils, with their horns, cloven feet, and eyes like goats, and their forked tails. Some of them had scales, like fish, and some of them were covered in black hair. I suppose they were like the Satan of the Bible, the one I had occasionally seen pictured, in, say, the Garden of Eden.

Two sweet cherubs flew overhead carrying a scroll on which was written, in red letters, with an arrow pointing downwards: 'Apathetic, Unbaptized, Lustful, Gluttons, Prodigal, Slothful, Heretics, Murderers, Suicides, Blasphemers, Pimps, Flatterers, Sorcerers, Hypocrites, Thieves, Traitors'. Below them the floor of the cathedral had opened up and steps led down to a funnel-shaped pit where stinking smoke was coming from. I knew where it was—Hell.

Some of the devils were much more unfamiliar. There were three-eyed, tiny blobby ones, like green jellyfish, which stuck to you. There were small blue ones with long arms and very, very long fingers, who specialized in stealing things, so that they would creep up on the people feasting and grab the food, from under the table.

There were others who only came up to my waist. They looked squashed—flattened faces, with their chins pushed down onto their chests, and no necks at all. I think they were the ones which people had tried to suppress, or pretend didn't exist. They muttered in some language I didn't understand, and looked very moody and stressed out, and would pinch people and even each other with metal fingers shaped like tweezers—very painful.

Some were dressed as women, but were men, and vice versa. Some had faces painted with mud, others were dressed in goat-skins and walked on all fours. All of these spirits were causing as much nuisance as they could.

One devil came up close to me, and held out a paw. He was quite small, with shaggy red hair all over his body but a completely bald head. He had donkey's ears and a donkey's tail. His feet were like a donkey's, too, but his paw was more like a monkey's—dark-skinned and slender. What did he want?

I took his hand. A smile came to his thick lips. He was lonely!

'What's your name?' I asked, not really expecting him to answer.

'Two words,' he said, in a thin, high voice.

'You have two names?'

He shook his head. 'Two Words.'

'Your name is Two Words?' I asked, still clutching his warm little paw.

He nodded. I looked into his pink, bloodshot eyes, which also looked like a monkey's.

'Why are you called that?'

'Speak two,' he said.

'You speak two words?'

'Only two.'

I laughed at this. 'But you have already said more than two words.'

'One time.'

'You only speak two words at one time?' I said, sniffing. His breath smelt of honey and spices, and I guessed he had been drinking the mead.

He nodded. 'Two enough,' he said.

'I suppose two is better than none at all,' I said.

'Watch trick,' he said.

'You want me to watch a trick?'

'I do,' he said.

Then he swallowed some air, then some more, stood very still, then burped a little tune and did a sort of skipping dance around me at the same time. I had never seen anyone burp in tune before.

I clapped my hands. This was the best trick I'd ever seen. He took a little bow.

'My friend,' he said, squeezing my hand.

'You could be my pet—I mean, my special friend, and come to see me sometimes,' I said, because he was starting to melt into the air.

'Perhaps. Goodbye,' he said, and burped again, and then he was gone. I wondered if I'd ever see him again. I hoped so. He'd really impress my friends, if only they could see him.

Then the riot police came to spoil the fun, and dog-wardens, and a few ambulances, and they restored order.

As soon as they rounded up the real dogs and real people, all the devils and ghosts and angels and spirits melted back into the walls. The flying cloud of bones, which had been hovering around above our heads, flew out of the door like a giant swarm of bees. It was peaceful in the cathedral once more. The Dog Whipper and I stood side by side, near the font, and tried to talk.

'I am so sorry about your mother,' he said. 'I thought it would be best if you saw her as she is nowadays. Not live just on memories. I know how hard it must have been for you.'

'You know nothing. You don't know me at all,' I said. I had been practising saying it, all bitter and dark, like poisoned chocolate.

He blinked, and said nothing.

'And you made my other friends go quiet. The angels no longer play for me. The Green Man, and the Acrobat Monk, they stopped appearing. The elephant with two pairs of ears, the archbishop with the power to make the sick well? Grumpy old Matthew, the music genius? Where is my friend Saint Sidwell?'

'Back up there on the east window, in the stained glass, where she has been for centuries,' he said, pointing.

'I mean the real Saint Sidwell. The one who talks to me.'

'Ah. Sometimes we grow out of these things. Sometimes we have what they call imaginary friends, I think. Then they disappear when we get older . . . ' he began to say.

'But there was nothing imaginary about her,' I shouted. I grabbed hold of his dog stick and was going to hit him with it.

Then Anthony came along. 'Who are you shouting at?' he said.

'Nobody. It's nobody,' I said.

'Good trick we pulled, eh, Bella? It's a shame the police came,' Anthony said.

'Yeah. Good trick. By far the best one yet,' I said, trying to sound enthusiastic, but my heart wasn't really in it. It was true what the Dog Whipper said. I was thirteen, now, nearly fourteen. I was getting old.

Twenty-one

'Goodbye, Bella, this is goodbye,' the Dog Whipper was saying.

We were standing in the dark outside the cathedral. It was late, and things had quietened down. Anthony had gone back to his Children's Home, and I was about to go back to the Special Unit. I was in a sort of daze, suddenly very tired.

'Won't I see you any more?' I asked, in a low voice.

'I don't know. I cannot know everything. But I do know that I must go to see your mother again. This is hard to say, but she needs me more than you, you know.'

'I agree,' I said, looking up at him. 'You're spot on, there. She needs you more than me. She's not right in the head, you know. Never has been.'

'I know. But she does love you, in her own way.'

I said my favourite swear words, in my favourite order. One beginning with A, one with B, one with C. I got as far as F.

'She does, Bella,' said the Dog Whipper. He was looking at me with his twinkling eyes. They seemed to shine with their own soft light, under the light from the black, wrought-iron street lamp, where we were standing.

'If she loves me, why does she keep disappearing? Ask her that, next time you see her. If she loves me, why doesn't she ask me anything about me, or write to me, or telephone me, or care about me? Ask her that!'

'Because when she gets too close to you, it hurts her. That's when she hurts herself—those false injuries, and going to hospital for no reason. All the ambulance trips, the drama . . . '

'Are you blaming me for all that?' I asked.

'Of course not. It's just that she can't do both—look after herself and you. Not when you are up close. She can only love you from a distance. Strange, isn't it? Hard to understand.'

'Very strange,' I said.

He started to say something else, some other explanation, like he was acting as some sort of go-between, but I put my hands over my ears and squeezed my eyes shut. He stopped.

'So, goodbye, Bella.'

'Leave me something,' I said.

'What would you like?'

'Leave me your stick—the one you whip the dogs with, or used to. I'd like to have your stick. To remember you by.'

'Of course. I have several spares,' he said.

He pulled it out from beneath his black cloak. He held it out in both hands, level. I don't know what sort of wood it was made from, but it was very straight, and light in colour. At one end it had a silver tip, held on by three silver rings which bit tight into the wood. At the other end was a metal handle. This gleamed with a bronze colour under the lamplight.

It was round and I could see that it would fit into my hand very nicely. The Dog Whipper turned the stick so that the handle was pointing towards me, and I took it.

It wasn't cold but quite warm to grip. I looked at the handle and there was an engraving on it, small but perfectly made, of a dog; the nicest, kindest looking mongrel, with big ears.

The Dog Whipper let go and the stick was mine. 'Thank you. Thank you,' is all I said. Then I put my arms round the Dog Whipper and hugged him nearly to death and he looked very embarrassed.

Then he walked away, back to the cathedral, out of our pool of light, and that was the last I have seen of him. I think I might see him one day, but it will be only if I am in big, big trouble, so I kind of hope I don't, which is hard.

I spent Christmas Day with Rosemary. She invited me over to her house, which is in the centre of the city, not far from the cathedral. She had candles in the window, a real Christmas tree tied up with ribbons and baubles, and with a tiny fairy on the top. No electric lights, only silver tinsel and coloured artificial fruits which she had made herself.

She had bought me just the right presents—a real silk skirt, a couple of CDs I had wanted, and had even dared to buy me some scent, which I liked. I thought it was a bit of a miracle that she could choose things I like. She went pink and looked pleased and said she had had to think about it hard, and get some advice from a friend's daughter who was nearly the same age as me.

Then it was New Year. The sales were on. I was out walking round the town, with no money to spend, but with my invisible stick—the silver-tipped one the Dog Whipper had given me. I enjoyed waving the stick around. It made me feel sort of powerful. No one but me could see it. I'd been out about an hour. That was when I saw Tarik again.

He was with his mum, Tina Bloor, and she was dragging him round the shops. He was four, now, and protesting quite a bit.

They didn't see me. It was in the biggest store in the city, on the third floor. Tina was looking for a dress and Tarik was sitting on a chair by the changing room, very bored.

I wanted to go up and say hello and sorry for what I had done, when he was littler, just try to say sorry, because no one had ever said sorry to me, ever. But I knew I mustn't. The courts had said I must never speak to him again. I hid behind a pillar and just stared.

He had the same lovely big brown eyes and shiny hair and his skin was still a lovely cappuccino colour. His little arms weren't quite so podgy, now. I could tell that when he was older he would be very handsome, and break lots of girls' hearts. I wondered if I could ever find a version of Tarik for myself but older, of course—a proper boyfriend. I had only recently begun to think of the possibility. Maybe it was because I wasn't so fat, and not so ugly.

Tarik sat with his feet not touching the floor. He was looking at the ceiling and I could hear Tina grunting, getting into clothes in the changing room, and see her checking through the curtains that he was still there. I suppose a mother gets super-anxious if her child's ever been stolen.

He was getting tetchy and said he wanted to get a drink. She said he could have one if he was a good boy— whatever that is. What she meant was, 'Sit quiet, stop whining, and wait for me.'

He twiddled his fingers, and sang himself a little pop song—one of those daft ones aimed at children around Christmas time. He must have just learned it.

He was wearing big boy clothes nowadays. Trainers, jeans, and a red and white football shirt—the local team. God help him, Tina was turning him into a sporty lad, and he was only four.

It seemed like an age that I was watching him. Then Tina came out wearing a most revolting party dress, pink and yellow, which made her look like a blancmange. One you would eat too much of, and get sick.

'Do you like it, Tarik? Do you like Mummy's new dress?' she said.

Of course he knew what was expected of him by now, and maybe he was thinking of that glass of Coke she had promised him if he played his cards right, because he said, quick as a flash, 'Pretty dress, Mummy. Very, very, very pretty,' which was just what she wanted to hear.

Who knows? Maybe she wanted the party dress because she'd met a new man who was going to be Tarik's daddy. Maybe. I would never know.

Then they went to pay for the dress and I sidled out down the lift and out into the street. I hoped that I would never see them again because it was too painful to remember how much I had wanted Tarik for my own and had been too young to know that I couldn't look after him, not like his mum, Tina, with all her tricks to make him good and keep him good. Bribes, threats, blackmail. The usual parent things. Useless as she was, she was his mum, and all he had, and that was that. And then that made me cry because I thought of my mum, and she was all I had, and she wasn't good enough, and that was *that*, and would never change even now she had discovered Jesus. It made Tina seem like a star mum, in the promotion zone, with mine in the relegation spot.

Then I rang Rosemary on my new mobile and luckily she was at home. I asked her to come out into the city crowds to see me, and asked her if we could have a cup of tea together, and she said we could.

So we sat, me, the slightly reformed tearaway bad girl Bella, and Rosemary, the posh old spinster with the sash at the cathedral, both lonely in our own ways.

She'd changed, in my mind at any rate. Once she was a silly old lady with a blue rinse, three cats named after angels, and a big purpose—to show you round the cathedral and so get you closer to what she thought God was. Now, she was a real person who was interested in me.

Next, who knows what?

'I want to ask you something very important,' I said, when the tea in my cup had reached the halfway point, a level I had set myself in order to get my courage up.

'Yes, Bella, what is that? Are you in trouble?' she asked.

'No. I'm getting totally boring. I haven't been in trouble for ages now,' I said.

'Are you short of money? I could lend you some,' she said.

'I'm always skint. No, it's not that.'

She waited, expectant, looking at me over her glasses.

'OK, here it is. Do you think you could ever, like, adopt me?' I said, and then wished I hadn't. I could hear all my dreams banging into each other in my head, like thunder clouds. Next, a flash of lightning would come, and strike me dead.

'I don't know. I would like to. I would really like to, Bella. But I don't know if the Social Services would ever let me . . . a woman my age, who has never had children . . . '

'They say they are going to make it easier, now,' I said, not letting her finish. 'They're going to change the rules . . . '

'We could try to find out. I don't want to raise your hopes, though. There are all sorts of pitfalls. But even if I couldn't adopt you, I would still stay in touch. I'm not going anywhere, Bella. I'm not moving. I'll always be in the cathedral on Tuesdays and Thursdays, and you know where my house is, and you have my telephone number . . . '

'Of course,' I said. 'I know all that.'

I thought of her in the cathedral, but not being able to see or talk to all the people I had met there, my friends. I tried to imagine never having spoken to the Dog Whipper, the Green Man, Saint Sidwell, all the others. Never having heard the patient mother pig grunting on the ceiling, while her piglets sucked, or seen the monk doing his acrobatics.

It was something which I could probably never tell Rosemary. She would never believe me. Or would she? Maybe if I got to know her really well. Really trust her not to disbelieve me, or call me crazy, like my mother does.

'I'm glad you know all that. I'm glad you know where to find me,' Rosemary said.

Then we finished our tea and walked out into the crowded streets and stayed together, people jostling us, all looking for bargains. But we didn't care for shopping and just enjoyed the walking and talking together, down to the canal, where we fed the swans and ducks with some bread Rosemary had brought with her.

Then we went our own ways, but not before making a date to see each other again, some day quite soon.

Other Oxford books

The Rattletrap Trip
Rachel Anderson
ISBN 0 19 271872 X

Being loved by Sarsaparilla made you safe and enfolded. And I tried to love her back, of course I did. But being loved by someone doesn't necessarily mean you like living with them all the time and putting up with their ever-changing life plans.

Sassy's latest scheme is to pile all six of her 'collected' children, from sixteen-year-old Elizabeth to baby Tilly (not forgetting Mr Churchill the hamster), into a rattletrap camper-van and move to an isolated farmhouse so they can get in touch with their 'mind-body-spirit' and learn to be at one with Nature. This means Sassy immersing herself in creating bizarre artworks while the children are forced to practise DD (domestic democracy) and I for I (independence for infants). Jewells does her best, learning (with Daniel's help) how to build a fire, chop wood, and prepare meals for the family with nothing but potatoes and swedes, but it is not long before things start to fall apart . . .

Last Chance
Patrick Cave
ISBN 0 19 275241 3

When Dad left and I came home from school and found his letter taped to the fridge I coped beautifully. The letter said he'd gone to St Kitts to live, that it was just something he had to do and sorry and look after the twins.

Julian's dad has run off to St Kitts, leaving him to look after his six-year-old twin sisters, with only a cash card and two Fuzzballs, the latest toy craze, to help him. Julian tries to cope on his own, but finds it hard to fit in his schoolwork and running practice as well, especially when the twins suddenly start behaving oddly. Julian is convinced it is the Fuzzballs that are causing the twins' erratic behaviour and tries to find out why—but no one else seems to have noticed anything. So Julian decides to stake everything on one last chance to prove he is right . . .

Marginaliens
Philip Gross
ISBN 0 19 271943 2

*'Mum . . . ?' said Enna as she came into the kitchen . . .
'Something . . . happened. Something scary . . . I was drawing,
and I drew this face, and it went all horrible, and . . . and then
it winked at me.'*

When she's fed up, Enna doodles. This time it's a scribbly,
hunchbacked, squatting figure—which suddenly winks,
speaks, and jumps off the page. It's Alive, with a mind of
its own. Enna can't believe what is happening. Her mother
is far too busy and too worried about the café to talk to
her, so Enna has to cope on her own—and then her little
brother finds the doodle . . . and disappears! What is Enna
to do when no one will listen to her? How can she get her
brother back? And will the doodle help her or is it just a
scribble after all?

Carried Away
Michael Harrison
ISBN 0 19 271907 6

There was a muttering and swearing in the front of the car in a voice that didn't sound like Dad at all. I pulled the rug off my face and looked cautiously out. It wasn't Dad driving . . . I had been abducted, carried away.

Dan tells his dad not to leave the car door open when he goes to get the fish and chips—and now look what has happened. The car has been stolen, and Dan is inside. Dan pictures all sorts of horrible things happening to him, but even he doesn't imagine what has really happened: he has been kidnapped by a girl of his own age. And when Jess uses his embarrassment at being carried away by a girl to blackmail him into helping her with more of her harebrained schemes, Dan is desperate to find a way out of her clutches. As Jess's plans seem to be getting them into more and more trouble, Dan has to find a way to save them both—and a way to finally break away from Jess . . . if that is what he really wants . . .

The Devil's Toenail
Sally Prue
ISBN 0 19 275310 X

I thought that if I held the devil's toenail in my hand, and I looked at it, perhaps, really close so I got cross-eyed—and if I concentrated really hard, then maybe I'd pick up this dark power and . . . and it'd be just so cool.

Steve had to leave his last school because of the bullying, and now, at this new school, he is determined to be part of the gang, to be in control. But to be accepted by them he has to do things he wouldn't normally do, things he is scared of. And then he finds the devil's toenail, a strangely shaped fossil, and convinces himself that it can give him power—power to impress the gang, to overcome his fears, and be what they want him to be—or maybe it'll help him just to be himself, whatever that is . . .

Home is a Place Called Nowhere
Leon Rosselson
ISBN 0 19 271914 9

She was tired of running, tired of roaming the streets. She seemed to have done nothing but run ever since she'd left Auntie Victoria's . . . All she wanted now was to go home, only she didn't know where home was.

Amina runs away from the only home she has ever known, desperate to find her mother and learn the truth about where she comes from and where her real home is. But where should she start looking? And what will happen if she is caught?

She meets up with Paul, another runaway, and together they enter the twilight world of asylum seekers, hiding from the police and from angry people who think all immigrants should be sent back home. But Amina doesn't know where home is and until she finds her mother and learns the truth, for her home will always be a place called nowhere . . .

Shopaholic

Judy Waite

ISBN 0 19 275275 8

A girl nudges her in the back. Taylor stiffens, wondering if she's trying to push in. But the girl is smiling. She nods at the dress, and says in a voice that is huskily warm, 'I would have gone for that if I'd seen it. Are there any more?'

Taylor can't believe that Kat wants to be friends with her. Kat is beautiful, confident, and two years older than Taylor, and is always surrounded by boys. But Kat seems to prefer going shopping with Taylor and Taylor thinks she has found a way to forget all her troubles. Life at home is terrible now Taylor's mother is so depressed, and it feels wonderful to have a way to escape and have some fun at last.

But then things start to spiral out of control and Taylor finds herself getting deeper and deeper in debt. How will she ever pay what she owes? And what will her mum say when she finds out? It is not until things come to a head that Taylor is able to break out of the web of lies and deceit that she has been drawn into and come to terms with the tragedy that changed everything.